3 9077 02134348 1   Gat

P9-CER-266

MYSTERY

ADA

Adams, Harold,
1923-

The man who met the
train

GAT-1

SEP 01 1988

$15•45   g 1595

DATE		

1/91 cue 4   LFC

GATES PUBLIC LIBRARY
1605 BUFFALO RD.
ROCHESTER, NY 14624

© THE BAKER & TAYLOR CO.

THE MAN WHO MET THE TRAIN

Gat

ALSO BY HAROLD ADAMS

MURDER
PAINT THE TOWN RED
THE MISSING MOON
THE NAKED LIAR
THE FOURTH WIDOW
WHEN RICH MEN DIE
THE BARBED WIRE NOOSE

3481

HAROLD ADAMS
THE MAN WHO MET THE TRAIN

A CARL WILCOX MYSTERY

THE MYSTERIOUS PRESS

New York • London • Tokyo

Copyright © 1988 by Harold Adams.
All rights reserved.

The Mysterious Press, 129 West 56th Street, New York, N.Y. 10019

Printed in the United States of America
First Printing: June 1988
10 9 8 7 6 5 4 3 2 1

Library of Congress Cataloging-in-Publication Data

Adams, Harold, 1923–
  The man who met the train.

  I. Title.
PS3551.D367M36 1988   813′54   87-20430
ISBN 0-89296-251-8

THIS ONE IS TO THE MAYORS
John & Barbara
Adrienne, Michele & Mark
My Other Family

GATES PUBLIC LIBRARY

THE MAN WHO MET THE TRAIN

1

I was wheeling along free and easy in my paid-for Model T on a narrow graveled road when I saw the brown Dodge with its front end crushed against the red clay bank just before a sharply angled right turn.

My first thought was the hell with it. There wasn't a sign of life or hope for it and none of it was any of my business. Unluckily, my foot reacted, I hit the brakes, the car coughed and died, and I heard the last notes of a meadowlark and the harsh cry of a child.

I scrambled from the Ford and ran for the wreck as the cry was repeated. I didn't look at the thing the steering wheel had driven through the fabric roof or at the other thing that had shot through the windshield. Bodies were huddled against the front seat which had been rammed up to the dashboard. Nothing moved. Then the cry came again. I jerked on the jammed door, gave up, kicked the last shards from the rear window, reached in to the nearest body, caught the shoulder, and pulled. From beneath it a small white face emerged, twisted in terror. At sight of me it straightened, the mouth closed, and the blue eyes blinked.

I reached down. She stared a moment, squirmed, freed her arms, grasped my hand, and came out like a cork from a bottle.

"Close your eyes," I told her.

She tried it, didn't like it, and opened them as I drew

1

her through the window. I pulled her face against my shirt and headed for my car. She murmured something like "Mamma" and was still.

I set her on the seat, cranked the engine over twice before it caught, climbed in, pulled the kid against my side, and headed for town as fast as the Model T would go.

It was early Sunday morning and there wasn't a soul on Main Street. I found City Hall, a red-brick two-story building in the center of town, parked at an angle in front, and climbed out. The girl whimpered and I leaned back in.

"It's okay, I'll be right back."

Her eyes puddled as she reached for me.

I looked around at the deserted street, sighed, picked her up, and carried her inside. The city clerk's office door was closed. The office across from it was open but unoccupied. I walked down a short hall, through a windowed door, and found two cells. One had a sleeper. He stirred when I hollered "Hey!" and after a moment sat up and stared at me painfully.

"Where's the town cop?"

The prisoner blinked, glanced around, and shrugged. "I ain't got him."

"Know where he lives?"

"Somewhere's on Cherry Street." He grinned at that.

I went back to the open office, found a wall phone, put my young friend on the desk beside me, took down the receiver, and gave the bell a crank.

The operator sang out and I told her my problem. She asked me to repeat the wreck location, asked where I was, told me to stay put, and rang off.

I picked up the kid, sat with her in my lap, and looked

her over. There wasn't a bruise or scratch in sight. I asked how she felt. She stared at me. I asked if her mother had been in the car with her. She nodded.

"How about your daddy?"

She shook her head.

When I asked if she could talk she stared at the floor.

"How old are you?"

She kept studying the floor.

"Show me."

After a pause she lifted her right fist and slowly unfolded four fingers.

"Okay. You're not just pretty, you're smart too, huh?"

That got me another blue-eyed stare. I suggested we walk out front and look around. She stood on my thighs and lifted her arms.

"Can't you walk?"

She shook her head.

When I pointed out that she could stand just fine, she shook her head again, so I said okay, picked her up, and headed out. The moment we reached the sidewalk a Model T newer than mine pulled up beside us and a stocky middle-aged man wearing a black suit, white shirt, and gray tie got out and approached, scowling.

He wanted to know if I was the fellow who'd called the operator. I confessed to that and wondered if that might be a crime on Sunday in Toqueville. He looked ready to charge me with something dire.

"What're you doing with Alma?" he demanded.

"Mostly I've been her packhorse for the last hour."

"She in the wreck you reported?"

"Yeah."

"She don't look damaged."

"She's the only one wasn't."

He nodded and said let's get out of the sun and led me into his office.

"Start at the beginning," he said when we were seated. "Who the hell are you?"

"What about the people still in the wreck?"

"Doc Leigh's on his way out there. If you told Emma right, he's probably pulling them out by now. Pokey Butts is on his way in his panel truck, so's they can get anybody to the hospital if that's needed."

That sounded like more organization than I'd expected from Toqueville and I let him know I was impressed before I laid out my story.

It was plain he wanted me to have been involved in the wreck. Locals always look for a foreigner to blame when natives suffer a calamity. After I ran down he sat staring at me a while, then looked at the girl in my lap.

"Stand her up," he said.

She turned her back on him and held her arms up to me.

"She's still spooked," I said.

She wore a yellow flower print dress that left her arms and legs bare. He leaned forward, looked her over without finding anything more than I had, and stared at me glumly for a few seconds after she'd settled back in my lap. "I don't get how come she's clamped onto a stranger like she has."

"She was probably scared and alone for a long time. Figures I rescued her."

"It's not natural. Hasn't even asked about her mamma."

"She did when we left the car."

"Maybe she remembers about her pa."

"What about him?"

"Walked into a moving freight one night. Less'n a year ago."

"Jesus Christ."

"You hadn't ought to blaspheme in front of her," he told me mildly.

He asked how come I was driving where I was so early in the morning. I explained I'd been heading for Sioux Falls and turned off the highway to sleep in a grove.

He allowed that'd be cheaper than a hotel and asked what I was going to Sioux Falls for.

"I do sign painting—figured I'd get work there."

He asked more questions and found out I'd come from Corden and had lived at the Wilcox Hotel. From his sideways glance I figured he'd heard about me, but he didn't ask for more and I didn't volunteer anything.

Finally, I asked what we were waiting for. He said the doc.

Church bells were chiming noon when the doc finally showed up. He was a tall gloomy man with sad eyes and worry wrinkles framing his eyes and mouth. He had no trouble detaching Alma from me. She obviously accepted him, but she kept a wary eye on his hands, probably watching for a thermometer, tongue depresser, or, worse, a needle. He went over her gently, said she was a brave, fine girl in perfectly wonderful condition, and planted her back in my lap.

"I don't think," I said, "I'm ready to take on a permanent attachment."

"Be patient. We'll get her sorted out in a little while, but for the moment she needs all the comforting she can get and you're it."

In that case I suggested we feed her and that was okayed. The four of us went down the street to Percy's

Place and slid into a booth by the front windows. The café had just opened and a few folks had dropped in fresh from church and all duded up to impress God. They stared at us a little more than was polite and I saw some whispering. In a small town news moves by something like osmosis, except it's faster than light and distorted as a broken mirror.

I asked Doc Leigh if there'd been any survivors and he said yeah, one, but he was in bad shape and we'd talk about it later when the little pitcher wasn't listening.

The café proprietor, a fat man named Percy McCleod, came around with a child's seat for Alma and I parked her on it. She wasn't interested in anything to eat but when I got her to try a malted milk she drank it down to the Scotch burp.

The cop, who Doc Leigh called Al, asked me roundabout questions until he grudgingly accepted the fact I'd shown up well after the accident happened, according to the doc's report. That didn't make him chummy but at least he wasn't hostile.

He was a little paunchy and a lot husky. He ate a hot pork sandwich with two glasses of milk and apple pie à la mode. That sounds like it all went down at once, and it damned near did. When it came to dining he had faster fingers than a riverboat gambler. Doc just drank coffee and let his sad eyes wander between us and around the café. People greeted him and he responded with a solemn nod, as if he knew what each of them would die of and didn't know how to beat it.

I asked them about the people who'd been in the car. Al glanced at Doc, who sighed, leaned forward on his elbows, and half closed his eyes.

"The driver was the youngest Hendrickson kid. Kenny. Just fifteen years old and a little wild—"

"More like big wild," said Al.

Doc shook his head. "He wasn't mean or irresponsible—just reckless and energetic. Anyway, the car was his father's. Ed. He's in insurance. The mother just about runs the Lutheran church. Kenny played baseball, football, and basketball. Wasn't big, but very aggressive—"

"And tougher'n bull gristle," said Al.

"The other boy in front was Kenny's older brother, Don. He was different; a good student, debated on our team that won second place at State a year ago—"

"Regular Philadelphia lawyer," said Al. "Slicker'n goose grease."

Doc gave him a squelching look that didn't take.

"So who was the woman?" I asked.

Al glanced at Alma. "Her mama, Winnie. Widow of the fella I told you about. Him that met the train."

"Where'd this gang been?" I asked.

"Dance, most likely," said Doc. "Whoopie John was playing over in Cranston. That's the direction they were coming from."

"How come the little girl was along?"

"Well," said Al, " 'cause Winnie wouldn't go anywhere without her. At a dance Alma watches till she gets tired, then falls asleep. No trouble at all."

"Must've gone over big with the guys that wanted to take Winnie home."

"Never slowed her I know of," said Al. "I think the guys'd gone for Winnie if she had triplets."

"Who was the other guy in the car?" I asked.

"Cody Jerome," said Doc.

"He's the only survivor, except for Alma?"

Al nodded. "Just like anybody'd figure. Cody more'n likely got the whole party going and of course he's the only one to come out of it. Except . . ."

We all looked at Alma, who was carefully flattening out the straw she'd taken from her malted milk glass. We watched as she rolled it up on the tabletop.

I looked back at the two men. "Tell me about Cody."

They looked at each other, and after a moment Doc nodded and Al leaned forward on the table.

"He's a comer. About twenty-two, maybe three. Handy with the girls, great at making up to the right people, ones that can do him good. His old man's been gone . . . my God, it must be twenty years. Ma used to take in washing a while. Later got a job as cook at the hotel. Cody moved out on her over five years ago, keeps hustling. Been running a candy and hotdog stand in a lot next to the bank for over a year now. Does a good business with the kids."

"Was he teamed up regular with—" I looked at Alma, who was suddenly staring at me, and finished, "Uh— girl?"

"Off and on," said Al. "Mostly on, I guess."

"Even before the husband met the train?"

"Before, during, and after. Cody's never been proud that way."

Alma tried to stand up in her seat and I caught her before she could tumble. As soon as she was settled in my lap she closed her eyes.

Al signaled for the waitress, ordered iced tea, got it, added three teaspoons of sugar, and stirred it with a long spoon so the ice tinkled. Alma slept.

"Some folks," said Al as he nodded toward the girl,

"figure she's Cody's kid. More likely Winnie didn't know one way or the other."

"I doubt," said Doc Leigh, "that she was that promiscuous."

"Oh, I never said nothing like that," said Al. "I just meant she screwed a lot."

I was about to ask where I could park my lap pet when the café proprietor ambled over and asked was I the owner of the Model T down the street. I admitted it was likely. He asked was I a sign painter, and I confessed to that too and asked if he figured that out because the sign on the back of the Ford said SIGNS PAINTED, and he said yes, would I do his windows, and I agreed.

"What'll I do with this?" I asked Doc as he and Al got up.

"I'll take her," he said.

Alma woke as I rose and the moment she caught on to the transfer she started to cry. Al, Doc Leigh, Percy McCleod, and two waitresses gathered around, trying to calm her, and were about as successful as all the king's horses and all the king's men. Doc finally suggested we take her to his house and see if she'd settle down where it was quiet.

We went up a walk flanked by tall evergreens and entered a fine brown house on a corner lot. His wife had comfortable curves, a narrow waist, and dark brown eyes that didn't exactly light up at the sight of me, but when Doc told her I'd pulled the little girl out of a wreck she took me in with a measure of approval. Doc's stumbling attempt to introduce me, after asking for my name, brought a tolerant grin to her warm mouth.

"I'll take her," she said, reaching for Alma. The girl was getting sleepy by then and the transfer went easily, but in a few moments she was reaching for me again. The doc's wife, looking a bit put off, handed her back and finally suggested I carry her upstairs and lay down with her in the back bedroom.

She led the way and watched as we settled down. Alma looked at me and said, "Daddy?"

I stared up at the brown-eyed woman standing over us and my face made her smile.

"No, dear," she said, "this is your Uncle Carl. Now go to sleep. He'll stay with you, don't worry."

I started to sit up at that and Alma cried, "No!" Her eyes began to flow.

"He's not going to leave you," said Mrs. Leigh, putting her soft hand on my shoulder, "don't worry."

"I've got a job downtown," I said.

"It can wait. She needs you now."

I glared at her and she looked back calmly while Alma hugged my arm and finally I settled back. If I didn't, I figured, this woman would trip me on the stairs, and if I did, who knows, one day the lady might get cozy.

Alma stopped leaking tears when I stretched out beside her and before long I thought she'd purr, but instead she just quietly went to sleep a few minutes after we were left alone.

I laid awake while memories of the car and the mangled bodies kept going through my head. Why the hell had this particular crowd been together and why hadn't there been any alarm about any of them missing all night?

And why was I in bed with a four-year-old girl I'd never been properly introduced to?

2

When I came downstairs half an hour later, Mrs. Leigh gave me a big smile, told me to go do my job and come back for dinner. She didn't tell me what a sterling character I was, so I couldn't tell her I'd only done it to please her and didn't learn whether that'd make any difference to her.

I hiked back to Percy's Place and painted his menu on the front windows. When I was finished and offered my bill, Percy griped that he could've got laid for less and I said that's the way things go when a man doesn't ask for the price in advance. He offered to pay me off in meals and I vetoed that.

"You do mottoes?" he asked.

I said it depended. We settled on IN GOD WE TRUST, ALL OTHERS PAY CASH, and I did the card for him and tacked it up over the mirror behind the cash register.

As he paid me off I asked what he could tell me about Cody Jerome.

"Just about all you'd want to know. Cody hangs around here a lot. The boy could sell iceboxes to Eskimos and condoms in an old-folks' home. Nothing special to look at; wears glasses, not tall or Tarzan, but he's got curly hair and bright eyes and a way about him. Girls can't leave him alone and he never fights 'em off."

"What's he do for money?"

He grinned. "Cody'd do anything for money. When he

11

was in high school he was the cleanup man and popcorn-machine operator at the movie. Made five dollars a week. While he was still a senior at school he ran a delivery service that went broke, so he talked Mr. Brundage into loaning him money to open the curb-service stand he's still got. Last year he hired five high school kids to play as a German band in the lot beside his place and he was going to build a platform there and get a dance band. He'll still do it if he gets over this accident."

"How long's he been involved with Alma's ma, Winnie?"

"Oh-ho! You already got that, huh? Well, nobody knows for sure but everybody wonders. Some say he's the pa, which means they were up to it five years ago—but it wasn't in the open much till Ellsworth walked into the train."

"How'd he happen to do that?"

"Drunk. He was mostly that way. A real lush."

"What'd he do besides drink?"

"Well, actually, he was a bookkeeper. Worked for Mr. Brundage over at the bank. You might wonder how a lush could hold a job like that, but Mr. Brundage said he was better with the shakes than most bookkeepers who never touched a drop. The real reason, I figure, is Mr. Brundage can't stand to hire a woman. He wouldn't hire one if he ran a whorehouse. Oh, he's got a wife, like everybody else, but long's he doesn't have to pay her a wage, they get along. Takes all kinds, huh? You do portraits?"

"Not even with a camera."

"You do good lettering. I like the shading. Seen guys do it so bad they got the sun coming from four directions. Always hated sloppy work. Where'd you learn?"

"Fella named Larry. What do you think's going to happen with the little girl?"

"Oh, somebody'll take her on, don't you worry none. If nobody around town can do it, they'll find a home say in Aquatown. She's a real cutey, eh? I'd keep her myself if I was younger, but my old woman's had six and isn't ready for another just now."

I left him to stroll up and down Main and was talking with a fellow in the soda parlor when Percy puffed in and said Judge Carlson wanted to see me.

"Why, what'd I do?"

"I don't ask him why he wants anything, I just do as he asks. You'd best do the same."

He gave me directions to the judge's office and I ambled over, climbed a flight of stairs, and went in through the first door on the right wondering why in hell a judge was at work on Sunday.

The judge was a big man with floppy white hair, a wide mouth, and brown spots across his forehead. His eyebrows were mostly dark and all bushy. He raised a puffy hand and waved me into a straight-backed chair facing his desk.

"I understand you pulled little Alma out of the wreck." His voice had the kind of rasp politicians get from yelling at large crowds.

"It wasn't hard," I confessed.

"It was a kind, responsible act. Many a stranger would've wheeled on by."

"I considered it."

He nodded solemnly and asked what changed my mind.

I crossed my legs, pulled out my fixings, and started

building a cigarette while taking him in. He watched without a twitch or a blink.

"I suppose I'm just naturally nosy."

He nodded, then slowly settled back, pulling his big hands off the desk and dropping them in his lap. "Officer Jacobsen tells me your name's Wilcox. You wouldn't be old man Elihu's son, from Corden?"

I assumed Officer Jacobsen was Al and said yes, I was.

"You've been in a lot of trouble in your time."

That was no news to me but I nodded and said I'd had my share.

"And some to spare, from what I hear. I've also heard that lately you've done some police work. Substituted for the regular policeman last winter, right?"

I confessed to that.

"So why're you on the road again?"

"Joey got well and took his job back. I used my money to buy a car and decided to go into the sign-painting business."

He pursed his lips. "I don't imagine that pays too well."

"I've been eating regular."

"Interested in a job for me?"

"You need a sign?"

He grinned tolerantly. "I've heard a bit about you. Things besides your fighting and problems with the law. Solved a couple murders, right? It happens I'm very interested in little Alma and her mother. I want to know what was behind this morning's tragedy, who was responsible. Would five dollars a day interest you?"

"I can make more doing signs."

"I'd pay expenses."

"Like what?"

"Any trips you'd have to make, long-distance calls, meals. Everything within reason. We could consult if anything unusual arose."

"Like buying information?"

"Within reason, yes."

"I don't know. I'm a stranger here—not too sure I could manage. Not on five a day."

"Let's not quibble," he said, frowning. "I'll give you seven-fifty a day. Take it or leave it."

"I'll take it. You know why Alma was in that car?"

He was startled by my sudden acceptance but after blinking or two said he had no idea why anybody was in that car *except* Alma. You'd know she'd be there if her mother was, that's just how it was with them.

"Didn't that bother her boyfriends?"

"Evidently not. She never lacked for one. Particularly Cody Jerome."

"I guess you don't like him much?"

"It's nothing personal. I just don't consider him a good influence."

We considered each other for a few seconds before I said I'd heard Winnie was widowed in the last year.

He nodded. "A tragic loss. And an awful waste. Ellsworth was an unusual man. Could've gone far. Brilliant. But weak. He couldn't face the world except through a drunken stupor."

"You think it was suicide?"

"I have no doubt of it."

"Was Winnie running around before her husband met the train?"

His bushy brows hiked up a notch. "Obviously you've heard the gossip."

I nodded. "You figure this car accident was Cody's fault?"

"I think it likely. He is an irresponsible young man. The episode is typical of him. Some claim he's been selling liquor to minors. He's never been prosecuted, but I believe you'll find it's common knowledge around town."

"You want me to pin that on him?"

"I want you to find out the facts about the car accident and anything else pertinent to that. Let the facts speak for themselves."

I said fine, I'd see what I could do. He got up, offered his soft hand, and shook mine warmly, even smiling a little, as if he'd just won my vote.

"You realize," he said, "this is not an open-ended contract. I expect results within a week."

"If I can't do it by then, I can't do it at all."

This time his smile was genuine. "Good, I like that. You can stay at Reynolds Hotel. Rooms are reasonable there and you can get a weekly rate."

I paused at the door. "One other thing. You going to let people know you've hired me?"

"I won't post it in the weekly *Herald*, but it won't be a secret. Officer Jacobsen will cooperate, I'm sure. So will everyone else. If anyone gives you trouble, let me know."

I wondered what kind of trouble he meant as I moseyed back to City Hall.

Jacobsen was hanging up his telephone as I came into his office. He'd been talking with the county coroner, who so far hadn't found anything unusual among the accident victims. They had been drinking some, except for Winnie, but not heavily.

I asked if he was surprised that Winnie'd been sober, and he said nothing that girl did or didn't do would surprise him much. He suggested we go out front and get some air and a moment later we were on the sidewalk, leaning against the brick wall and gawking up and down the sleepy street. The only action in sight was at a gas station a block east where a service man was filling the tank of a black Packard. He finished up, wiped the windshield, took money, and disappeared into the station. The car pulled out and drove by us. The driver looked like the son of a bulldog bitch and peered at us from under beetled brows. He gave Jacobsen an ivory smile and Jacobsen waved back politely.

"That's Mr. Brundage," he told me, "our banker. He ain't pretty but he's a very smart fella."

I said oh, and waited for more.

"He ain't very tall, either."

"How's his weight?"

Jacobsen glanced at me. "Not a lot, but he carries a good deal in this town. If you meet him, call him 'mister.'"

"Who's more important around here, him or the judge?"

He didn't answer until he'd scratched the back of his head and smoothed the hair down. "I guess you could say the jury was still out on that."

After a few more minutes of admiring the empty street he asked me what the judge wanted to talk to me about. I thought some before answering. It seemed likely he had a good idea already, or if he didn't, he'd soon get the word. Either way it didn't seem likely he'd be tickled pink about me being hired as a private snoop, since it might suggest the judge didn't have all that much faith in his town cop.

Finally, I outlined my assignment.

He nodded and thought a moment. "What's he know about you that makes him think a sign painter'd be a good snoop?"

"He knows what you told him—that I've been a cop and done some private work the last couple years."

He considered that a few seconds before shaking his head. "I guess he knows what he's doing, but I don't get it."

The trouble was, neither did I.

3

When Mrs. Leigh answered my knock, Alma was at her side clutching a Raggedy Ann doll with both arms.

"I told her you'd come back," she said with a smile.

Alma looked shy and offered me the doll. I took it, moved inside, gave Ann the eye, and guessed it had endured a lot of hugging.

"I'm just making salad for dinner, come join us."

I handed the doll back to Alma and trailed them into a big square kitchen lined with dark cabinets and counter space that'd turn our hotel cook green with envy. There was a café-style booth up against the south wall and a window overlooking a small green backyard with a dinky round flower garden in its center.

Alma slipped into the booth with me right behind. I turned down lemonade and accepted coffee. When I reached for my tobacco sack Mrs. Leigh shook her head and I shoved it back in my pocket. She started tearing up lettuce in a bowl and asked what I'd been up to.

"I saw a man named Brundage and learned he likes to be called mister. Are you always called missus?"

"Call me Annabelle."

"Not *the* Annabelle?"

"No, I'm not dead and I never came from a kingdom by the sea, but I've heard smart cracks about it most of my life."

I looked at Alma and said I hoped she and I were going to get along. She looked back solemnly without making any promises.

Still, I thought, maybe dinner'd be okay.

Annabelle asked where I'd seen Brundage and I told her and then she wanted to know why the judge had sent for me and I began wishing I'd just published that notice in the *Herald* he'd mentioned.

The front door opened and closed and I looked for the doc, but instead a brunette appeared in the door. She was a slimmer carbon of Annabelle, with a wider mouth and brown eyes with flecks of color that made me think of Wisconsin in fall. Annabelle introduced her as Evangeline, the kid sister.

"I guess your ma liked poetry," I said.

"She was gooney about it," said Evangeline as she sat down across from me. A wicked grin widened her mouth. "Tell us about the murders you solved in Corden."

"All of them?"

"Sure. Especially the one where the woman killed her husband's girlfriend. Why wasn't that justifiable homicide?"

"It's hard to make a case for that when you knock off three people and make a try for the town cop plus me."

"Oh, you turned vindictive when she tried to do you in?"

"Well, it seemed like there'd ought to be an end to tolerance somewhere along the line."

"Uh-huh. Like pacifism ends when the villain attacks me. Is it true you owned a black snake and wore it around your waist so it scared people to death in saloons?"

"Only once. Mostly I wear a belt."

"From what I've heard about your drinking, it seems like you wouldn't be fond of snakes."

Doc Leigh's arrival ended that subject and a few minutes later we were putting on the feedbag. It was pork chops and great brown gravy, mashed potatoes, peas and baking powder biscuits, all topped off with devil's food cake and fudge frosting.

When I'd downed all that and staggered outside for a smoke, Evangeline joined me on the back step. Her brown eyes drifted over me.

"What're you going to do about Alma?"

"What do you mean, what am *I* gonna do about her? She's not mine because I pulled her from a wreck."

"Don't you like her?"

"Well, sure, but her conversation's limited."

"I thought men liked that in a woman. You prefer talkers?"

"Is there some special reason you're on me, or are you always like this?"

She laughed, showing her bright small teeth. "As a practical joker, you'd ought to catch on when you're being kidded."

"I gave all that up when I figured it was sneaky and mean."

"There was nothing sneaky about that snake."

"But it was mean. Scared hell out of guys and even made one woman wet herself. I felt lousy about that."

"I bet you laughed at the time."

"Damn near died."

She took a deep breath when my smoke drifted her way and I asked if she wanted a cigarette. She shook her head.

"Ma always said only hussies smoked, and I believed

her so long I can't let myself try even yet. She was crazy but awfully nice. Is your mother living?"

"She thinks so."

"What's that mean?"

"Quite a lot. When did yours die?"

"Mothers don't die, they pass on. Mine did it about five years ago. I don't suppose yours approves of you much?"

"Much, hell. Never. How come you're not asking me what brings me to town and why I'm staying?"

"I figure you're interested in Annabelle, or at least in her cooking. But I was going to get around to the rest, so how about it?"

"It'll take a while—want to walk a ways?"

She said okay, went inside to tell her sister, and a moment later we were strolling toward the business district while I wondered if she was interested in me or just getting out of the kitchen cleanup.

Toqueville is flat as a steamrollered mouse and about as interesting. There's a bakery, grocery store, pool hall, beer parlor, creamery, and grain elevator. We passed a funeral parlor two blocks from Main and about five churches scattered around. The town didn't have anything like the number of trees in Corden and its park had a grove of spindly elms planted in rows straight as recruits on a Marine parade ground. I asked Evangeline if they had a swimming hole anywhere and she said no, was I in the mood?

"I just wonder what kids do for fun in the summer."

She said they played ball in the lot south of the park, tossed cherry bombs in cars and outhouses, and played hide-and-seek in the sandpit west of town. A lot of them went to Bible schools.

I asked what the bigger kids did.

"They borrow their folks' cars and get themselves killed looking for excitement. Where are you going to be staying?"

I wondered how she knew I was but said the Reynolds Hotel. She suggested it might be a good idea to go over and sign in so I'd be sure of a room. It didn't seem likely to me that Toqueville's hotel would be doing a brisk business but I saw no reason not to humor her, and a few minutes later we entered a square dull lobby with a few chairs and little light. There were two men parked in rockers, one gray and wizened, the other a young towhead. Evangeline sailed up to the registration counter at my side before it dawned on me she was staging a shocker for the locals. The young towhead left his rocker and came around to face us on the far side of the counter. He was stocky, and his face was red heading for purple. He was working hard not to look pop-eyed.

"I need a room for about a week," I said.

The young man looked at my partner and asked did I want a double?

I turned to Evangeline and she chickened out.

"It's only for him, Arnie," she said. "He just had dinner at Annabelle's and I walked him over."

The young man's red began to fade.

I signed in, said I'd be back with my bag, and walked Evangeline outside.

"I thought you'd given up being a joker," she said. Now she was the one looking sunburned.

"Who was joking?"

She gave me a quick sidewise glance and decided to drop the subject.

"Is this Arnie guy sweet on you?" I asked.

"Uh-huh. He's been that way since I kissed him when we were in grade school."

"*You* kissed *him?*"

"It was a phase I went through."

"I figured there was something up when he started looking like a stoplight. You trying to use me for something?"

"Don't be silly. I was just trying to embarrass you. Arnie's nothing to me."

I said I saw, and thought I did.

"How about Cody Jerome, what do you think of him?"

She frowned at me. "Why'd you ask that?"

"Percy told me he was the city charmer and lady's man. I figured he must have made a play for you."

She flipped her wrist casually and said yes, as a matter of fact he had. "Actually, he taught me how to drive a car. Daddy nearly had a conniption fit when he heard about it. Cody's a very good driver—I learned a lot. But we only really dated a couple times. He walked me home from a dance once and another time we went to a movie. He tried to move too fast, and I wouldn't put up with that and he didn't come around again. I didn't care."

I overlooked the lie and asked to see where she'd gone to school and she walked me to a big old yellow-brick building in the middle of a bare block. The town water tower was west of it and cast its shadow across the walk leading up to the double front doors. We strolled up the walk, through the shadow, and sat down on the front steps.

She'd liked high school, maybe even loved it; gone to all the dances, did some illustrations for the school annual in her senior year, and had just missed being prom queen.

"I pretended I didn't care," she confessed, "but immediately hated the girl who won, and before that she'd been one of my best friends. It wasn't jealousy, though. I mean, she got so *condescending* and *gracious* it just drove me wild. Does that make me sound like a crumb?"

"It sounds like you were both pretty normal." I asked if she'd known Alma's mother, Winnie.

"No. She was never part of my crowd. We all thought she was wild, even before she went to the altar preggers. Actually, there wasn't even an altar—she was married by a justice of the peace in Aquatown, pretending it was an elopement. As if her parents cared. Her father was too sick to pay attention and her mother was crazy."

"Was Winnie a lush?"

"I don't think so. She smoked—the only girl I ever knew who sneaked puffs in the girls' room. I saw her doing that. But I never saw her drinking."

"Was she in your class?"

"She was never in my class anywhere—but if you mean my grade, no. She was one year ahead. My English teacher, Miss Stensrud, told everybody Winnie was quick. She was crazy about smart kids and the only teacher Winnie ever was polite to. Winnie got smart with all the rest."

"How'd Stensrud like you?"

"We got along, but she never bragged to anybody about me."

I asked what Winnie did besides smoke and have a kid.

"Well, most of this past year she was a live-in maid at Uncle Cal's."

"With Alma?"

"Of course. Uncle Cal sort of took them in just before Ellsworth had his accident."

"You sure that was an accident?"

She straightened and turned her head. "Why'd you ask that?"

"Just wondered. I've been drunk a time or two but never got so smashed I walked into a moving train. Maybe one parked, but not moving. They make a hell of a noise, you know?"

"Well, everybody, or almost everybody, says it was an accident. He got sort of like a zombie sometimes. A few people say he wanted to commit suicide but was too drunk to get in front of the train in time."

"Nobody saw it happen?"

"Not that anybody knows of."

"What'd girls like you think of Ellsworth?"

She tipped her head back and sighed. "Actually, he was kind of—I don't know—romantic? I mean, he was mysterious in a way, and tragic."

"Good-looking?"

"Yeah. In a way. He had a long slender nose and real deep dark eyes and black eyebrows and hair. When he smiled he showed beautiful teeth. I wasn't around him any, but I heard that he said strange things that seemed to amuse him and confuse people. He was kind of sarcastic, I guess. That's what they say."

"What's your Uncle Calvin do?"

"He's the judge. Judge Calvin Carlson."

"Ah. So who's his live-in maid now?"

"Well, I suppose I am. I'd prefer to think I'm taking care of him. That's what they say when you're related, right?"

"And not paid."

"Oh, he pays me. Uncle Cal's not stingy."

I switched to asking about the kids in the wrecked car, but she didn't know much about them except that their parents were stiff-necked Lutherans who were probably more upset to hear their kids had been drinking than that they'd been killed. Finally, she said she'd better get back to her sister's place before she got into a stew.

Annabelle didn't appear to be stewing when we entered her kitchen but she was definitely high on warm. If Evangeline noticed it she kept it to herself.

Alma wanted in my lap the moment I sat down, and I accepted her since I couldn't smoke in Annabelle's realm and needed something to occupy me. When it was her bedtime I carried Alma upstairs and once more found myself stretched out beside her.

"Story?" she said.

"Did your ma tell you stories?"

She nodded.

"I'll tell you one if you tell me one."

She thought about that for a moment, then shook her head sadly.

So I told her about the time my old man and ma had been trapped three days during the blizzard of '88. They had run out of water the second day and found that melting snow took forever. My old man never was a patient type and insisted he'd go out to the pump and get what they needed. It was snowing and blowing so wild he couldn't see a thing and Ma wrapped his head with a scarf, bundled him into sweaters, overcoat, and boots, and sent him out. He felt along the house to the corner where the clothesline was hooked and followed it to the barn. From there he moved by dead reckoning to the pump about a quarter of a rod away.

When Ma told the story it seemed to take a week for the old man to make the trip, and I suppose it seemed that long to Alma. And of course the old man made it and everybody lived happily ever after.

Alma liked the story so much she didn't ask any tough questions, like how come the well wasn't frozen. In fact, she was so quiet I thought I'd bored her to sleep but then she asked for another story.

I said I only told one a night.

She asked where her mother was.

I said I didn't know, but she was okay, don't worry.

She asked where heaven was.

Since I'd be the last to know I suggested she check with Annabelle in the morning, she'd probably have all the details.

To distract her, I asked if she'd known any of the people in the car she'd been riding in. She didn't answer. I named the Hendrickson boys and asked if she'd known them. She shook her head. Cody's name made her frown.

"You knew him but didn't like him?"

She nodded.

I asked why and she just frowned. I asked if he pinched, punched, pushed, or yelled at her and she shook her head again. I guessed he'd probably monopolized Winnie's attention when he was around and never told Alma a story.

Finally, she fell asleep and I went downstairs to exchange polite talk with Annabelle and the doc before heading back to the hotel. Evangeline had disappeared and no one mentioned her. I left, wondering what the hell.

4

Sounds in the hall woke me around eight and my first thought was relief that I'd had no night visitors. The Reynolds Hotel looked like a place with bedbugs. When Pa had taken over our hotel in Corden it had been alive with them, plus mice and cockroaches. The dog we brought promptly got fleas and I was surprised I didn't get crabs, but that was probably because the former cook went out with the crumby mattresses and cracked washbowls that Ma discarded on our arrival. We spent four weeks at war with varmints and vermin. Maybe that's what soured me against hotel management at a tender age. And maybe that was lucky. Without all the pests I might've grown up like my old man and never seen the Pacific or the islands, California, Montana, Utah, and everyplace else I traveled on the bum.

I might've turned out respectable.

As was, on this particular morning I woke, dressed, shaved, and ventured out to look over the town, and in the early light found my dusty Model T with all its windows broken and the tires slashed.

I walked around it twice while two yokels watched, grinning. When I stopped and stared at them their faces turned solemn and sympathetic.

"Where's the town garage?" I asked.

The taller one tipped his head toward the east.

I thanked him and headed that way.

Simpson's Garage was a long sagging gray clapboard building half a block off Main. Simpson was gray, balding, and paunchy. His hands looked like gloves you've forgotten outside over a rainy night.

I described the condition of my car and asked what it'd cost to fix it. He thought that over about a week and named an amount only twice what I'd paid for the flivver secondhand. I thanked him and asked how much it'd cost to store it in his garage a week or so.

He said two bits a day.

I began to wonder if he was the one who'd banged it up, since it looked like he was going to be the principal beneficiary, but I didn't question him about it because he looked like a man who only answered questions he could put a price on.

I went over to Percy's and the moment I parked my buns on a stool the man came around and sat beside me.

"Hear you had a little accident," he said cheerfully.

"That was no accident, and who told you?"

"Ellie Borden, my cook. Saw your car on her way to work. Says it doesn't look like hail damage."

I agreed that seemed like a safe guess. I've seen some wild hail in my time but none sharp enough to slash tires.

"You think somebody's trying to tell you something?"

"Could be. But if they wanted me to leave, why cripple my car?"

"They probably figured you'd hop a freight."

I gathered there'd been a little talk about me around town.

I ordered two eggs over easy, bacon, and coffee, and while putting them away asked if he knew a fellow named Arnie over at the Reynolds Hotel.

"Sure. He's old man Reynolds' cousin. Working

through the summer. In the fall he'll go back to Aberdeen Normal. Gonna be a teacher. You get close enough to Evangeline so you think Arnie did your car?"

"Would he do it?"

"Huh-uh. If he busted anything it'd be you. Old Arnie's a hero type, like Hairbreadth Harry, the fella in the funnies."

I'd never met one of those so, after paying for my breakfast, I wandered over to the hotel. Arnie wasn't at the counter, but an old lady on duty told me he was out back, burning trash. I found him poking at a smoking pile in the bottom of an oil drum. When I said hi he glanced at me, gave the fire another poke, put the poker down, and faced me.

"Yes?"

"You know which car out front is mine?"

"It's the one with the tires cut and the windows broken."

"How do you figure that happened?"

"Probably somebody with a tire iron and a hunting knife."

"Yours?"

He folded brawny arms across his manly chest and shook his head. "I don't own either."

"Got friends that do?"

"I believe in Polonius' advice to Laertes—'neither a borrower nor a lender be.' Did Evangeline tell you we're close friends?"

"I figured that out watching you go through six shades of red when we walked in last night."

He demonstrated a couple shades right there but kept his arms folded. "I didn't smash your windows or cut your tires and if you call me a liar I'll knock you down."

"Fair enough. But if you're ever serious about knocking a man down, don't tell him while you've got your arms folded. You could wind up on your ass. You willing to have a cup of coffee with me?"

He considered the proposition, unfolded his arms, said why not, and walked with me back to Percy's. Percy took us in with bulgy eyes but kept his distance when I ignored him and guided my young friend into a booth.

I asked if he'd heard the judge had hired me, and he said yes and everybody knew why.

"He'd love to prove Cody Jerome was responsible for the accident. Not so much because he hates Cody—he just doesn't like him much—but because he's Brundage's favorite. The judge'd do about anything to embarrass Brundage."

"Why's that?"

"Oh, it goes way back. When Brundage first came to town they were fairly thick, then there was a hassle about some property the judge sold to Brundage. It was supposed to have been for development but Brundage found out it had sand and gravel and turned it into a pit, which of course ruined the value of the other land the judge owned nearby, and then the judge found a couple cases in favor of people Brundage sued and they've been at it hammer and tongs ever since."

I asked what he knew about the accident Sunday morning and the kids involved. He said not much about the accident and little about the Hendrickson boys. Everybody knew Winnie by reputation. He'd never danced with her but had seen her smoking at Percy's and dancing with other guys at the Playhouse, where everybody went for Saturday nights. He admitted he'd had words with Cody Jerome after the villain had tried to make time with Evangeline. I suspected he had threatened to thrash him within an inch of his life, but he didn't say so.

"Cody," he told me, "is another potential Brundage. Has the same greedy instincts and sneaky charm, but of course he's better-looking and taller. The only thing I don't understand about the accident is why he was with those brothers. He's got his own car, so why ride with them? I suppose maybe something went wrong with it and he talked the boys into giving him and his woman a ride. He's very persuasive, you know."

"Why do you think Winnie was stuck on Cody?"

"I don't know why any of the girls around here have been stuck on him. He seems to have a Svengali-like hold on them—especially Winnie."

"Why's the banker interested in Cody?"

"I don't know. Maybe sort of a father feeling—like he sees him like a son and gets a kick, sort of secondhand, in the way Cody gets girls."

"You think Alma's Cody's kid?"

He considered that and finally granted it was hard to imagine that the little blond girl came from Ellsworth.

"From what I've heard and seen," he told me, "I'm almost inclined to think Winnie conceived the little girl all by herself. There's a term for that—escapes me . . ."

That was fine with me.

I paid for his coffee and we walked out into the bright sun and a steady breeze that smelled of dust and heat. He wished me luck very politely.

The bank was on a corner and I had to climb three steps to get in the front door, so I knew it was a high-class establishment. The tellers were fortified behind barred windows, but south of them was an area protected only by a fancy little fence all varnished and shiny. Way back in the corner I spotted Brundage behind a huge desk. He looked like something a native might carve with the wrong kind of rock and bad tools. His thinning hair was oiled flat and parted in the middle.

A young guy looked up from a desk immediately behind the fence and asked, very doubtfully, if he could help me.

I told him my name and said I wanted to see the boss.

He looked faintly alarmed but got up and went back to the man, who glanced past him at me, blinked thoughtfully, leaned back, and nodded his broad head. The clerk returned looking relieved, opened the gate, and waved me in.

The man didn't rise or offer to shake hands but nodded at the straight-backed chair beside his desk. His eyes attacked mine. I crossed my legs, dug my makings from my shirt pocket, and started building a smoke. His patience held out as long as it took me to finish and reach for a match.

"So," he said, "you're the ex-convict Judge Carlson's hired to gather gossip."

"The emphasis," I said, "is on 'ex.' I'm also an ex-cop, you know."

"In the tradition of the West. If you can't tame them, hire them to tame their ilk. The basic nature of cops and robbers is just about the same."

"Yeah, but how'd a banker know that?"

He frowned a second but got his grin back quick. "Bankers got exposed to both types a lot. How much is the judge paying you?"

"How much does a bank president make?"

"More than a snoop."

"Yeah, well, you've been at your racket longer than I've been at mine."

"You'll never live long enough to make what I do."

"You got a crystal ball, or was that a threat?"

He leaned back and folded his chunky fingers across his middle. "Why on earth would I threaten you?"

"Damned if I know—yet. But my car got messed up last night so it seems like somebody's worried about what I might find out and that's made me sensitive."

"Yes, you look sensitive. You think you're going to prove Cody was responsible for the accident?"

"I'll try to find out if he could've been, yeah."

"That's a stupid assignment. Who's going to be helped by putting the blame on Cody? It isn't as if he's come off lightly himself, you know."

"I don't make the judgments, I just ask the questions and look for the answers. You got an interest in Simpson's Garage?"

His eyebrows rose and he asked why I'd want to know that?

"Well, like I said a minute ago, my car got smashed up last night sitting all by itself on the street and I haven't been able to figure out who'd profit."

He stared at me a moment, started to laugh, then sobered and shook his head. "You'd better be kidding."

"Some. But can you tell me why anybody'd do that?"

"With your record, there's probably lots of people, but I'll admit it's hard to imagine anyone in Toqueville doing it. Maybe somebody wants to find out just how smart you are."

"I suppose you've heard the stories going around that Cody sells booze to minors?"

"You do switch around, don't you? Yes, I've heard that. It's hogwash. Cody's too smart to make a business of anything that risky. He's no fool, and believe me, I don't back losers."

I didn't remind him of how far behind Cody was at the moment—it didn't seem like he'd appreciate that. We sparred around a little bit more before I got up to leave and he took the last shot.

"You'd best put your car in Simpson's Garage nights—he doesn't charge much."

I thanked him for his thoughtfulness with almost no sarcasm and left.

5

I met Al Jacobsen on the street and walked with him toward City Hall. He seemed genuinely upset about what had been done to my car.

"Nothing's ever happened like that before in Toqueville. I just can't believe any of our people'd *ever* do a thing like that. It just don't make sense."

Nothing much had since I'd hit town. I asked if he knew any guys besides Arnie who were sweet on Evangeline.

"Well, I suppose there're lots of 'em—she's a very fine-looking girl. But don't you go suspecting Arnie. Why, he's a student, knows more words than you can find in a dictionary. . . ."

We went into his office and sat down to smoke. I asked about Evangeline's mother.

"That was a high-toned lady," he assured me. "Went to a classy girls' school back East. Started our town library, even ran it the first few years. Be there every Wednesday night and Saturday afternoon. Didn't get what you'd call a lot of business but she was happy just sitting in the middle of all them books. Fine-looking woman. Lotsa fellas dropped around and pretended interest in books when the fact was they didn't even read funnies."

"What'd her husband do?"

"Old Sam Carlson was a lawyer and real estate man.

He and his brother, the judge, were partners. About half
what they sold went to Mr. Brundage when he first came
to town."

"Where'd he come from?"

"Chicago."

"Why to here?"

"Well, the story he tells is he was taking a train to the
West Coast and it hit a cow just east of here and stopped
quick while Mr. Brundage was in the aisle going to the
can and he got thrown down and wrenched his shoulder
bad. They took him off the train and brought him to
town, and Doc Leigh, who'd just started practice then,
he treated him so fine he decided this was where he
wanted to go into business and a year later he opened his
bank right there on the corner of Main and Second."

"Where'd he get his money?"

"Inherited it. His pa was a big Chicago banker. Before
the Crash, you know. The way Mr. Brundage tells it, his
pa got religion and thought Chicago was a sinful city and
wanted his son to get out and raise a family in a decent
place, and so he'd been traveling around and the accident
seemed foreordained. That's how he put it. And besides
meeting Doc Leigh he got acquainted with Judge
Carlson, who was only a lawyer then, and they hit it off.
According to Mr. Brundage, the most important people
in a man's world are his doctor and his lawyer, and he
found both the first day he hit town so he settled in."

We moseyed over to Percy's and drank coffee while I
pumped him some more and then I went over to
Simpson's Garage and made arrangements to have the car
fixed. He told me it'd take a while, he wasn't set up for
all the glass I needed. Considering the cost of the job it

seemed to me he could've cheered up a notch, but if he was excited about getting rich he kept it a secret.

It was noon by then and I headed for Annabelle's. She accepted my arrival as if it were expected and we sat in the kitchen, which is my favorite room in any house, and gabbed some. Alma's appetite hadn't picked up much. She didn't insist on sitting in my lap but leaned close and kept quiet. We ate baloney sandwiches and drank iced tea.

I asked Annabelle if she'd heard the story about how Mr. Brundage came to settle in Toqueville. She said yes and she gave it all the credence it deserved. That slowed me a tick or two, and I asked if it wasn't true, what *had* brought him around. She let me know she was about as interested in that as in trying to figure out why ostriches quit flying. I didn't know they'd ever started but felt that line wouldn't lead anywhere and mentioned that I'd heard Brundage and the judge had been buddies in the beginning.

"The Carlson Brundage hit it off with was my father, Sam, not the judge. If you haven't got that straight you'd better take a good look at the rest of the education you've been getting in this town."

"The judge was never chummy with Brundage?"

"Hated each other on sight. They've been playing king of the hill from the beginning. You'd hardly think Toqueville was worth an argument, let alone a feud."

I thought that over and asked if the judge was married.

"Widowed. Wife died about five years ago. Flu."

"So Winnie and Alma were living in his place?"

"Uh-huh. It raised some eyebrows but not as much talk as you might expect. Uncle Cal's over fifty and he's never been a lady's man. When Winnie moved in she was barely twenty."

"That was right after her husband was killed?"

"Actually, it was a little before. Some say that's why Ellsworth killed himself—because she left him. I never believed that."

I asked where Doc Leigh was and she said he'd gone to a farm east of town to deliver a baby.

"How does Evangeline feel about this Arnie fella?"

"She doesn't see him as any knight in shining armor. Of course we don't have a lot of those around, so maybe she's not even expecting one." Then she took a sip of iced tea, put the glass down, and gave me a direct look. "Don't go making any plans for her yourself."

"I'm not the marrying kind," I assured her.

"I never thought you were. You're the one-night-stand kind. What Evie wants is a tall blond man with a lot of money, and she's not going to settle for a half-pint saddle tramp."

That came sudden and mean enough to stagger me some and my only comeback was to take a sip of iced tea, look thoughtful, and put my arm around Alma.

Annabelle's eyes narrowed as the little girl leaned into me. "She's served you awfully well, hasn't she?"

"Huh?"

"Alma. She latched onto you from the start and you've been able to parlay that into acceptance all around town."

"Hey, come on now—you're the one talked me into staying—"

"Oh sure. You were easy to coax, weren't you?"

I looked down at Alma. She'd eaten the half a sandwich Annabelle had made for her and was nibbling on an icebox cookie. She caught my gaze right away and lifted her blue eyes while still chewing. I wondered if she'd ever smile. And I wondered why Annabelle had suddenly turned so hostile. My first notion was she was jealous of her sister, but that seemed stupid and I groped for something else. It didn't seem likely she figured I was using the kid to make myself accepted. On the other hand, I knew it wasn't the sort of advantage I'd overlook if it dropped in my lap. And of course it had.

"If I really wanted to use her," I said, "I'd take her for a walk through town."

"Yes. Where do you plan to go?"

"Down Main Street."

"I'll get her a bonnet."

The bonnet was near as blue as her eyes and too big, but Alma accepted it without a murmur and took hold of my hand as soon as we were outside. She kept looking up, hoping I'd carry her, but said nothing and finally started taking things in as we strolled along the sidewalk. The sun was high and hot and the wind made her bonnet flap. We didn't meet anyone as we walked east and I thought some of stopping for coffee but decided against that and headed for the park. There we found shade and sat on the ground to watch boys playing softball on a dusty diamond under the broiling sun. They played the kids' way—everyone versus the batter. As soon as he was put out the catcher took his place and he went out in the field until he worked his way back through the basemen, pitcher, and catcher. They called it Work Up.

After a while they decided it was too hot and drifted over to our shade. Alma crawled into my lap.

The boys were between thirteen and fifteen. A red-haired Swede asked me if the little girl was Alma and I said yes. The redhead squatted and said hi to her. She turned away.

"Kinda spooked, huh?" the kid said to me.

I nodded.

"Was there blood on her when you pulled her outta the car?" asked a towhead.

"No. But let's not talk about it, okay? She hears real good."

"They say the Dodge was doing eighty when it hit the bank," said another kid.

"Where'd you get that?" asked the redhead.

"Well, that's where the speedometer was stuck."

That brought on a sharp debate that didn't enlighten anybody and finally I butted in and asked if they knew how come the Hendrickson brothers got teamed up with Cody and Winnie?

"Sure," said the Swede. "Cody got in trouble with old Bo and didn't dare go back to his car because he knew Bo'd be waiting for him, and got the Hendricksons to give him a ride back. He just left his car on the street in Cranston. It's still there."

"What kind is it?"

"Chevy. Shove it or leave it."

"You figure Ken was showing off and went too fast?"

"He might've. He was a crazy driver. Most the time Don wouldn't let him drive and his old man *never* would."

"You guys know Kenny pretty good?"

"Sure. He used to play here with us."

"He was a lousy hitter," said the towhead.

"He didn't miss the bank," said the gang wit.

That brought a heavy scowl from the Swede and guilty grins to the rest.

"You gonna find out who caused the wreck?" asked the wit.

"What makes you figure it was caused?" I asked.

"Well, if somebody didn't, why'd the judge hire you?"

"When I figure that out I'll let you know. You guys think there was something funny about the accident?"

"Naw," said the Swede. "We just figure it was Cody's fault. He probably gave Kenny a bottle of booze for the ride."

"He pay off that way a lot?"

A couple of the kids said yes but the Swede didn't back them up and the others just looked thoughtful.

"You don't look like a private eye," the towhead told me. "You look more like a fighter."

"You see a lot of private eyes in Toqueville?" I asked.

He'd seen movies.

"I've been a cowboy. Do I look like any you've seen in movies?"

"Yeah," said the wit, "one of the guys in a black hat."

Even I had to laugh at that, but they enjoyed it more than seemed polite and I got annoyed enough to tell the kid if all he knew was what he saw in the movies he had a hell of a lot to learn.

Eventually, everybody but the Swede wandered off, but he stayed with us when Alma and I headed back toward town.

I asked if he knew anything about Cody Jerome.

"Like what?"

"Did he sell liquor to kids?"

"Not to anybody I know."

"And you know most of the guys around, right?"

"Sure."

"You think he might've got the Hendrickson brothers drunk?"

"He'd offer if he wanted a favor. Kenny'd take it. Don probably wouldn't. But Kenny was driving."

"You knew him pretty well?"

"Sure. He was a real wild one. All kinds of guts."

I didn't tell him what I'd seen on the steering wheel that had shot his body through the car roof. "I suppose," I said, "you know all about the feud between Judge Carlson and the banker?"

He shrugged. Obviously it didn't interest him since it only involved old people.

"You ever hear that Cody might've been a father?" I asked.

He admitted he'd heard that.

Neither one of us looked at Alma, but she raised her head and glanced at the Swede and back to me.

"Is it pretty common talk?"

He nodded and avoided Alma's blue eyes.

Alma pulled on my hand and when I stopped she raised her arms. I picked her up.

"I heard," said the Swede, "you got a way with the ladies. You start 'em early, don't you?"

"Red," I told him, "this little lady's not for kidding about. You're smart enough to understand that, okay?"

It took him a few seconds to think about that and decide not to be offended.

"I heard," he said suddenly, "that once you whipped a carnival pro in Corden when the carnival came through."

"No I didn't. I just lasted out the three rounds."

"My old man says you knocked him down twice."

"I tripped him once and he went through the ropes when he thought he had me and missed."

Wearing the pillows they'd strapped on my hands to start the brawl, I couldn't have knocked Alma down. The only good thing about the gloves was they were big enough to hide behind, so all I had to worry about was the referee who hooked me twice with elbows before I realized he was the biggest danger to me in the ring. I made up my mind by the middle of the first round that I'd never fight again except barefisted and unroped.

We came to the soda parlor and I offered Red a drink, which he accepted. He and I had root-beer floats while Alma sucked a milkshake. The proprietor was a tall white-haired man everybody called Pop, although to me he looked more like a maiden aunt whose mustache had gone out of control. If he enjoyed his work he hid it well.

Red had just finished his float when the judge came in and headed our way. He nodded at Red, gave Alma a big smile, said, "Mind?" and took the fourth chair at our table without waiting for an answer.

Red thanked me for the float, tipped his head toward the judge, and drifted.

"I see you're getting a broad perspective of Toqueville," said the judge as he glanced around at Pop, who came bustling over. "Gimme a cherry Coke, Pop."

Pop dredged up an expression that bordered on cordial and took off.

Alma pushed her empty glass away, climbed down from her chair, and stepped over close enough to lean halfway across my lap while she watched the judge out of the corner of her eye.

"You've made quite a conquest," the judge told me.

"Don't ever remember her warming up to a man before."

"You figure her mother had something to do with that?"

"Probably. I must say you're the most unlikely surrogate I've ever seen."

I've been considered unlikely in lots of ways but figured he'd think I was bragging if I said so and let it lay.

"So what'd Brundage have to say?" he asked.

"Wanted to know what you were paying me."

He grinned. "He offer to top me?"

"Not yet. You think he might?"

"He would if it'd keep you from finding out what I want to know."

"He didn't make an offer."

"Probably thinks you're not getting anywhere."

Pop delivered his Coke and the judge took a sip, while watching me thoughtfully. Alma started climbing into my lap and I helped her up.

"She always been quiet?" I asked.

"Not like lately. Talked to her mother a deal but not much to anyone else. She's not simple, if you're wondering about that. Should be around other kids her own age. It's not natural for a child to spend all its time with grown-ups."

I agreed that was so and asked him how he came into all the property he owned.

"Shrewd choice of parents. Just about all of it was inherited. Not as much as some folks think, but enough to give us a healthy start."

"Us. You and your brother?"

"That's right. Samuel. You've heard about him?" He said it very casually.

I nodded.

He brushed his mouth with a paper napkin and smiled at me. "What'd you hear about Sam?"

"He was a lawyer, and your partner a while back."

"Right. Senior partner. The smart one. I'm afraid I have to admit he was most responsible for our business in this town."

"You got holdings in other towns?"

He twisted on the chair, crossed his thick legs, and leaned one elbow on the table. "You're quick, aren't you? Yes, I have picked up a few properties elsewhere. Including Cranston. Nothing great."

"How?"

"I doubt that's relevant to your current investigation, but to satisfy your curiosity, it came through a mortgage foreclosure. Some property came available at a good price because the forecloser didn't wish to handle it and I could."

I nodded, rolled a smoke, and said I'd heard he had a bookkeeper who was hired away by Brundage.

He frowned and put both elbows on the table. "Brundage didn't hire Ellsworth away, I let him go. Got so I couldn't stand the sight of his hangovers. He never drank on the job but he swilled so much on his own time he was never truly sober. Alcohol flowed through his veins and pickled his brain by inches. I just couldn't watch it any longer. We had a talk and I told him to straighten up. He asked for a week off and I said if he went on a toot he needn't come back, and the next Tuesday he was working for Brundage. People said he went for more money, but that was never the question with Ellsworth. That had nothing to do with it."

The memory of the desertion made him sore and he

scowled at his glass, suddenly came to himself, sat back, and gave me a careful smile. "I hear you took my niece for a walk last night."

I said yeah and asked if he and his brother were still partners.

He shook his head. "Not since I moved to the bench. Have to worry about conflicts of interest and all that. Besides, there's not much business these days. Not in real estate or anything else, except crime, fornication, and boozing. Your kind of business." He said that with a smile but it was awfully thin.

"All that brings you your business now, Judge. And it sounds like you think Toqueville's become a little Chicago. Is that how it looks from the bench?"

"I exaggerate a trifle," he said, "but you got a hint of what's happening when someone vandalized your car. Surprising things happen in a town when there aren't enough jobs and those working get their wages cut. Hope disappears."

I told him I'd talked with a citizen who thought all that was the banker's fault.

He twitched angrily and leaned forward. "Sounds like Arnie Bridstand. He thinks everybody'd be happy if the government ran everything. Socialism, or worse."

"You figure bankers are okay?"

"They're like everybody else, doing their best for themselves. There's no big conspiracy to gather all the cash in the world into their vaults or personal accounts."

"Not even Brundage?"

He gave me a cozy smile and leaned back again, making the chair creak dangerously. "I'll tell you about Mr. Brundage. He's the only child of a Chicago pirate who got religion and offered to bankroll his little boy if he'd get out of the city and make an honest living. Brundage isn't just a banker, he's a promoter, a manipulator, a man with a basic hatred for, and fear of, women. He didn't marry a woman, he contracted for a maid he wouldn't have to pay a wage. I'm absolutely astonished that the people of this town have generally failed to see through him."

"I guess you're not great pals."

"I hope you don't think that observation impresses me with your deductive talents. And while we're on that, what progress have you made?"

"Nothing to brag about. But I've still got a few days."

"Well, you're not likely to learn much useful from me or your young companion there." He struggled to his feet. "I suggest you begin to stir about."

He left without paying for his Coke, and when I paid my bill Pop said nothing about it, so I figured judges were maybe like cops and got special privileges.

6

I took Alma to the Leighs' and shared a roast beef supper. Evangeline joined us, saying the judge was eating with some cronies, and after we'd finished I sat just outside the screen door behind the kitchen and smoked while the women did the dishes.

"What're you going to do next?" asked Evangeline as she wandered near the screen while wiping and shuffling a stack of saucers.

"I'm thinking about a trip to Cranston."

"What good'll that do?"

"Won't know till I go. But can't go without my car."

"You could take a bus," said Annabelle.

"No," said Evangeline, "the hours are ridiculous."

I asked what they were and she wasn't sure. "It doesn't matter," she said, "I'll take you in my car."

Annabelle's silent reaction to that was about heavy enough to thump on the floor.

"Hey," I said, "that's the best offer I've had all week."

The women finished the dishes in silence, and then Evangeline came out and suggested we take a walk.

We went west a ways while I rolled my fag and she stayed in step with me, watching as I lit up. The match flare showed her pale face, dark mouth, and soft hair.

"Tell me what's going on," I said. "You trying to rattle your big sister?"

"Maybe," she said, giving me a flirty glance. "Or maybe I'm just taken with your hungry hobo eyes."

"What do you know about hobos?"

"Nothing, I guess."

"The difference between a hobo and a tramp is, hobos travel and tramps beg. Sometimes tramps travel, too, because they get shoved along. Hobos now and then beg, but they travel because they want to."

"Is that how it is with you?" she asked, tilting her head. "Are you looking for a dream?"

"I only expect dreams when I sleep, and I don't much find them even then."

"No illusions?"

"Sometimes I get a notion a woman I've met will take me as I am. That's about it."

"Actually," she said, "you're too old for me."

"I was probably born too old for you."

"You think I'm childish?"

"A little. Annabelle says you want a tall blond man, with money. Is that right?"

"Annabelle lies now and then. She's always been jealous of me. You interest her, you know. She's never known anybody like you. She's going to try and manage you—she's very good at that sort of thing. Managing, I mean. Do you think she's too heavy?"

"Nope. Just well-rounded."

"She'll get fat when she grows older. She takes after Uncle Cal."

"She's in her prime now."

"You think I'm skinny?"

I turned her way and made a walking inspection. "No, I wouldn't say that at all. You're like a thoroughbred colt, all full of promise."

"I'm no colt, I'm a full-grown woman."

"No argument—you look better than fine."

She decided I was teasing her and walked along, swinging her arms freely.

"Maybe," I said, "I'd better go to Cranston alone. You come along and guys won't pay me any attention at all."

"Don't worry, I'll bring a book and read in the car."

We had reached the scraggly park by then and sat down on a bench facing the deserted ball diamond. Off beyond the lot we could see dim lights in houses facing our way and crickets were sawing away in the grass.

"I might have to see a lot of people," I said. "It could take quite a while."

"I'll bring a long book. Maybe two."

"You that bored with Toqueville?"

"Yes! Why're you going on with all this? Are you afraid?"

"No . . ."

"Then let's drop it and go back so you can get Alma to bed. Everything's all settled."

And so it was.

7

"**A**nnabelle tried to make me take Alma along," Evangeline reported as we headed out of Toqueville the next morning. "I told her if she thought that'd provide a chaperone she'd better remember how well it worked when Alma went along with Cody and Winnie. Imagine! She wanted me to baby-sit all day."

"Well," I said, "she wouldn't have given you any trouble."

"She wouldn't have given *you* any trouble. You'd be off all day."

The twenty-mile drive took us over a meandering graveled road through low rolling hills and a couple sloughs before we reached plain flat-out prairie with mostly sunburnt corn and a little wheat that waved and rustled in the steady wind. Overhead was all pale blue with nothing for mix but sun. Behind us dust rose and whipped away into the fields.

Evangeline'd recovered her good humor overnight and drove a steady fifty with both hands on the wheel and her eyes mostly on the road, which ran a straight line to the end of the earth. She asked about cases I'd worked on before and I told her a little, leaving out the mistakes and building up the luck. I could see her sorting it out, deciding what to believe and what was gas. She had a way of asking innocent questions that turned out to be needles poked into balloons I'd blown up.

"Don't you ever carry a gun?" she asked.

"Never. Shot one once. It wasn't mine and I only used it to get the guy's attention. Can't hit anything."

"You'd rather punch fellows around, wouldn't you."

"Yeah. It's more personal and less permanent."

"One day the bad guy won't let you get close enough and you'll get killed."

"Why is it everybody I talk to lately keeps giving me warnings?"

"Well, Carl, it's a dangerous world you're in, but you don't seem to take it very seriously."

Cranston was a carbon copy of Toqueville, only maybe duller. The dance hall was on the second floor of a building housing the Legion Club Rooms, so proclaimed by a badly lettered sign over the front door. There were rickety steps up to the dance hall entrance. I could see from the street it was padlocked.

Evangeline said she'd been to dances there a couple times. "It's owned by Miller. He also owns the pool hall and the beer parlor."

I left her in the car by the town park and ambled back to the beer parlor. The man behind the bar gave me a raised-eyebrow look as I drifted over and asked what I'd have. I ordered a beer and looked around. The only other patron was an old-timer sitting near the middle of the bar nursing a shot glass and a bottle of beer.

I remarked that it was hot out and got no argument. I explained I was in town to check on an accident in which some Toqueville people got killed after visiting Cranston and could they help me any? The bartender said no. It came out flat and uncompromising, while his eyes met mine and didn't blink.

"You own this place?" I asked.

He nodded.

"Own the dance hall, too, right?"

He nodded again. His brown hair had a cowlick that bobbed with his head movement and at each question his wide mouth arched down at the corners a little more.

"You heard about the accident?"

"They didn't get drunk here."

I grinned easy. "I hadn't asked that one yet. But since you know it wasn't here, where else would it have been?"

He shrugged.

"You know Cody Jerome?"

"I know what he looks like."

"How about the Hendrickson boys?"

He shook his head. The small blue eyes watched me suspiciously as he leaned on the bar. He admitted Winnie Ellison had been in the bar with Cody last Saturday night and she'd had Alma along.

"I threw them out. Don't allow kids in here."

"They'd never been in before?"

"What difference does that make? What the hell's it to you?"

"I'm working for Judge Carlson. You know him? He wants to learn a few things."

"Yeah, he would. Wants to pin the whole business on Cody, right?"

"All he asked me to do was find out what happened."

"So you're his snoop, huh? Hell of a way to make a living."

"I don't suppose it pays as well as selling booze to minors."

"I don't!" His cowlick nearly flipped off.

"Who said you did?" I grinned at him.

The old-timer chuckled. He was a small man with a prune face and a two-day stubble. I couldn't imagine how he could shave that face at all. His watery blue eyes swung from Miller to me, back and forth, like a kid waiting for two other kids to fight.

I pulled out my fixings and started building a smoke. "My name's Wilcox," I said to the old man. "What's yours?"

"Art Elevitch. Seen you doing rope tricks in a Aquatown speakeasy six years ago. You was drunk."

"I must've been if I was doing rope tricks in a speakeasy."

The old man chuckled again and tipped his head toward the bartender. "This fella Wilcox," he said, "he could make that there rope do anything but talk. Loop was steady as a hoop, high or low, stepped in and out of it and took it to the floor and just about to the ceiling, made it big and small and snared the waitress carrying a tray without spilling a glass or touching anything but her middle. Good as a magic show."

His memory wasn't pure and he didn't mention how mad the waitress got or that somebody stole my lariat while I was busy drinking all the booze my audience'd paid for.

Miller began to simmer down a little, not because the old man's talk fascinated him, he hardly paid any mind, but because we didn't exchange any more nasties and he wasn't able to brood on one thing for long. Eventually, he let out he'd heard that Cody and Winnie had danced up at the hall while the little girl slept in the empty cloakroom on a cot brought over from the hotel. He insisted he never saw the Hendrickson brothers or got any reports about their drinking. He also claimed Cody hadn't had so much as a sniff in his bar.

"Where'd Cody get booze in town?"

"No place. This town's tight."

We gabbed a little more and Elevitch asked me what I'd gone to prison for. I asked which time and he said either and I told him about the rustling and the jewel robbery, neither of which quite came off, and he snickered and chuckled and looked at Miller, who showed sudden interest. Pretty soon he admitted he'd served some time himself back when he wasn't much more than a kid.

After that we got along like old cellmates. He told me I should talk with Sarah Singer and a fellow named Bo Grummen. They'd been talking a lot with Cody from what he'd heard. In fact, he said, the story went that Cody'd made a play for Bo's girl Sarah and Bo had called him out. He didn't know what'd come of that.

He gave me Sarah's address and I went back to the park and peered into Evangeline's car. She was sitting sideways across the front seat with her legs up and her back against the door. She looked up when I poked my head in the open window.

"I'm going to talk with a woman. Want to come along?"

She said why not and hopped out.

The address was on the seedier side of town, two blocks east of the shopping district. A gray-haired heavyset woman answered my knock.

"Gone to the Cities," she answered when I asked for Sarah.

"When?"

"Last night. Her and her fella. Eloped."

"Who's the fella?"

"Cody Jerome."

I blinked and said, "You sure?"

"Of course. Sarah told me herself."

"It's not likely. Cody Jerome's in the Aquatown hospital. Had a bad accident Saturday night."

Her eyes opened wide. "Accident? What happened to Sarah?"

"She wasn't with him. When'd you talk to your daughter?"

"Saturday night—she called from downtown. Was Sarah hurt?"

"She wasn't in the car. The only woman there was Winnie Ellison."

"That hussy!" She hissed that and glared at me for a few seconds before the doubt returned and she looked at Evangeline without seeing her.

I asked her to tell me about Saturday night, and after a moment she sighed and leaned against the sill.

"Well, she called first, then came by for her suitcase and some clothes. I wanted to talk with her, but she just kept saying there wasn't time and she'd call or write and not to worry. She was awfully excited."

"You sure she didn't say the guy she was going with was Bo Grummen?"

She jerked erect. "Certainly not! I'd have stopped her, believe you me."

"What's wrong with him?"

"He's"—she shook her head, looked past me at Evangeline and then beyond her—"evil. A mean, brawling, bullying lout." The description didn't satisfy her, but she stopped, frustrated and afraid.

"But Cody was okay, huh?" I said.

She smiled. "Oh yes. He came to get Sarah once, and another time after, I met him on the street and he was just as polite—a kind smile and a warm word. Gallant. That's his way. Not many like that around. Comes from a good family, you know. Folks go to parties in Aquatown and entertain a lot. Elders in their church."

"Where'd you hear that?"

"Oh, Sarah told me all about him. You sure he wasn't the one she went with?"

"Positive."

She looked so sad I felt I should leave her alone, or maybe lie a little, but I found myself asking if she knew where Bo Grummen worked.

"He's a laborer, when he gets around to it. Works for that fellow who builds all the highways. Art Zaun. Another no-good."

I asked where I could find him and she said only God knew, so I went inside and called the telephone operator, who told me Zaun was in Elrod. I got him on the phone and asked if Bo Grummen was still working for him.

"Nope. Took a leave to get married."

"Know where he is?"

"Cities somewhere."

"Got the address?"

"Hell no, I'm not the shivareeing type and there's no other reason I'd want to know where he was."

"He coming back?"

"I wouldn't bet on it."

"Why not?"

"Well, Bo's a man with big ideas. Wants to start at the top and work up, you know?"

"Think he'll make it?"

"He might, if he doesn't get caught killing somebody."

"Hotheaded, huh?"

"Bo? What he is, is cold-blooded and bloody-minded. That is one spooky son of a bitch, but don't ever tell him I said that."

"Why do you say it? What's he done?"

"I haven't got time to chew the fat, mister, I got a road to build."

He hung up.

I suggested that Evangeline drive me around to City Hall for a talk with the city cop. Maybe he could give me Bo's address.

We found him having a smoke out front when we drove up. Evangeline introduced us and left. His name was Tom Purvis. He was a lanky guy in a shabby gray suit with baggy knees and a tie that was close to black and had been under quite a few meals involving gravy. It didn't surprise him any to hear Sarah's ma hadn't heard about the accident; he said she never talked with neighbors and only knew what showed up in the weekly *Clarion*, which wouldn't be out till Thursday.

"She could even miss it then," he said, "since all's she reads is the society page. Who had a party and who went to it."

"She quite a partier?"

"Naw. Just reads about 'em. How come you didn't swing by here when you first hit town? You talk with Joey in Corden, don't you?"

I had to admit I did. Sometimes it seemed to me half my conversations in Corden were with the town cop for one reason or another, but I didn't go into that and apologized, saying I should have come around. I started to ask him about Sarah and Grummen, but he was still stuck on proprieties and interrupted me.

"I know you been a town cop for a while, so you'd ought to know when a fella wants to check around a town he talks with the law first. The trouble with you, Wilcox, is you was a hobo and an outlaw too long. When you come to changing your ways, you got to change them all the way. Okay?"

I granted him that and asked if he knew about Sarah and Bo Grummen running off together.

He said no, he didn't, nobody told him nothing. He was deeply offended.

I asked what kind of a guy Bo was.

"Got a mean streak a mile deep. Strong's an ox. Played football for Cranston High about five years back—about got us penalized to death. I mean, you couldn't look hard at the bastard without he'd try to cripple you. Been like that long's I can remember. I can't figure why Zaun'd hire him, but I'd bet you he keeps him on 'cause he's scared to fire him no matter how he sasses or bullies other men on the crew. He knows, like everybody else, Bo's not a man you cross more'n once."

"He got any friends?"

"Oh sure, fellas just like him. There's Tuck Tucker, he's a two-legged bull. Maybe not really deep-down mean, like Bo, but he goes along with whatever Bo wants. Works at the creamery, mostly wrestling milk cans. Then there's Arlo Fisher. Arlo works in his old man's bakery. He can stick his head between hundred-pound sacks of flour and lift two easier'n I'd lift a couple pillows. Then there's Mac McCall. He works part-time for Miller at the beer parlor and is the bouncer at the dance hall. I guess you might say he rassles beer kegs and drunks. They all played football with Bo."

I said I'd mosey around and meet these fellows and he offered to show me the way. I thought that was kind, figuring how hard they'd be to find in this town, but he wore a kindly expression as we strolled down Main, squinting against the bright morning sun.

The creamery was cool, smelled of sour milk, and had a cracked concrete floor. We found Tucker in the back room, watching a cream separator spin. He was wearing a white jacket, stained pants, and a white-billed cap. Purvis greeted him and introduced me. I caught a flash of hostile blue eyes from under sandy brows before his attention settled on the cop.

"Mr. Wilcox here," said Purvis, "wants to talk with Bo, but he's not at work. Know where we can find him?"

"What's he want of Bo?" demanded Tucker. Freckles covered his broad nose and wide cheeks, and when he spoke I saw a gap between his front teeth wide enough to spit a cherry seed through.

"What difference does it make what he wants?" asked Purvis.

"It might make a lot."

"Tuck, you either know where he is or you don't. All's this man wants to know is what happened Saturday night when Cody Jerome and some friends was in town. You know what happened later—what *we* want to know is what happened early. You go to that dance?"

"Yeah," said Tucker, as an older man came in from the next room. I guessed he was the boss because Tucker glanced at him nervously. "Yeah, I went. So'd everybody else in town. Bo and Sarah were there and took off for the Cities. Gonna get married." He suddenly glared at me. "You wanna talk to him, take a train."

"Where's he gonna be in the Cities?" asked Purvis. His irritation was growing and it was plain they'd clashed before.

"How'd I know? He didn't give me no address and I don't plan on sending a wedding present. They'll be back when they get to it."

"How come he didn't tell his boss when he'd be back?" I asked.

He gave me a cold stare. "Probably figured it was nobody's damn business."

"Married men usually want to keep their jobs."

He shrugged. "Bo'll manage."

The older man moved closer and asked Purvis what was the trouble.

"No trouble, Ed. We're just trying to find a friend of Tuck's."

Ed looked at me, but Purvis didn't introduce us and led me back out into the sunlight.

"You and him had trouble before?" I asked.

"Me and Ed? No. Me and Tuck, some. I'll tell you, if old Bo never comes back, it'll suit me. Tuck and the others'd just be a nuisance without him, but he comes back, one day there's gonna be big trouble. I know they run a poker game weekends and got some other things going. All got more money than their jobs pay. I'll nail'em one of these days." He said it without enough conviction to convince either one of us.

The big problem for small-town cops is they know everybody. That doesn't make them fond of every citizen, but it means every time they come down on a culprit they're also touching a friend or a relative of somebody straight and life gets complicated. A few local lawmen are willing to accept antagonism and even ostracism as the price of the job, but it tends to make them isolated and mean. Most of them settle for breaking up fights and restoring stolen property. A guy like Corden's cop, Joey, can go down the middle road, enforcing the law within reason, soothing relatives of strayed souls, and getting in touch when it's necessary to keep the townsfolk feeling comfortable.

I guessed Purvis was betwixt and between. He had the inclinations of a tough cop but couldn't handle the complications and avoided deep digging. You ask too many questions and you can wind up with more answers than you can handle.

"Maybe," I suggested, "it'd be simpler if I just wandered around on my own and talked to these guys. You being the town cop and all, they get kind of defensive and standoffish. Maybe I can get straighter answers as just another Joe."

He thought about that seriously. His brow furrowed and his mouth drooped until he finally nodded and agreed. "But you tell me what you find out, right?"

I gave him a lying smile. He pointed me toward the bakery and I was on my own.

Arlo Fisher was leaning against a glass show case just inside the front door of the bakery. One of his huge square-knuckled hands gripped a coffee mug, the other a doughnut. My eyes hit his chest low and rose past his broad bony shoulders, thick neck, strong jaw, and up to the bright brown eyes. Behind the counter a fat lady in a white apron over a Mother Hubbard dress gave me a million-dollar smile. I grinned and ordered half a dozen doughnuts, figuring I might make a friend.

"You order a dozen and you get one free," she told me.

"What do I get free with half a dozen?"

"Six holes."

I said that'd do, told her my name, and said I was trying to find out what'd happened the night the youngsters from Toqueville got killed.

The lady's smile vanished quicker than a magician's handkerchief and she turned solemnly to the young man. "Tell 'im, Arlo, what you told me yesterday."

Arlo drank from his cup and looked down at me. "You a cop?" he asked softly.

"I been a lot of things, but right now I'm just trying to find out what happened."

"What happened," he said, "was those kids got drunk and crazy and drove too fast on a road they didn't know. That's what happened."

"You saw them drunk?"

He finished his doughnut, washed it down with coffee, and nodded.

"Where?"

"At the dance hall."

"You saw them drinking?"

"Nobody's allowed to drink in there. But they were drunk, all right. Especially the little guy."

"Kenny Hendrickson. He was fifteen."

"I don't care how old he was, he was sozzled. Him and his older brother."

"Where'd they get the booze?"

"Cody Jerome. Everybody knows about him."

"You ever get any of his stuff?"

"I can get my own."

"You ever see Cody give or sell any booze?"

"Bo did."

"You know where he is now?"

He smiled. "Probably the Cities." He didn't know where in the Cities and he didn't know when Bo'd be back or whether he'd ever return to his highway job.

"I hear Cody Jerome tried to hustle his girlfriend," I said.

"What's that got to do with the accident?"

"That's what I'd like to know. It seems funny Sarah was dancing all night with Cody but wound up leaving to get married on the same night Cody nearly got killed."

"Sarah didn't dance with him all night. Just a couple times. She was just trying to make old Bo jealous."

"She got the job done, huh?"

"Seems like. They took off to get married."

"Uh-huh. But before he went, maybe he and his old football buddies followed Cody and his friends a little close when they started back home?"

"What'd they want to do that for?" His face was all innocence.

"A little excitement, who knows?"

"Nobody knows," he said with a bright smug smile.

"How'd Bo get to the Cities?"

"In his Graham Paige."

"That's a pretty big car."

"Bo's a big fella. With big friends."

The fat lady watched us with growing concern, but finally a customer came in and she moved off to wait on him.

I said to Arlo I guessed they'd done okay in football back when they played together. He admitted that was so. A few more questions brought out the fact he'd played end and thought it was the best position on any team. He even told me he liked defense better than offense. "I like to hit." He laid a lot of emphasis on that while looking down at me, and I said that made sense and asked how they'd done against Corden in the games they'd played.

"Beat 'em two out of three I played in."

I got the story of two of those games before it dawned on him I was more interested in getting friendly than in learning the history of his football career and suddenly he clammed up.

I picked my bag of doughnuts off the counter, wished Arlo luck, and walked back to the car, where I left the doughnuts with Evangeline.

It was just past noon when I entered the bar. The long room was cool, dark, and held the smell of tobacco and old beer. My eyes adjusted to the dim light and I spotted Tucker, the guy from the creamery, standing at the bar toward the back. Across from him was a chunky red-haired Irishman with a button nose, shaggy eyebrows, and a perfect chin for an uppercut. They watched me approach. I glanced around and saw the old-timer, Elevitch, asleep at a table in the far corner. I parked on the stool one down from Tucker and asked for a glass of beer.

"Can you pay?" asked the Irishman.

I dug out a nickel and placed it on the bar. He drew one, wipe off the foam, and shoved it over.

"I guess you're McCall," I said.

"And you're Wilcox, the snoop from Toqueville."

"Actually, I'm the snoop from Corden, but just now I'm working out of Toqueville. I hear you guys were riding in Bo's Graham Paige last Saturday night—or Sunday morning.''

Tucker glanced at Mac, who kept his eyes on me.

"You got it wrong," said Mac. "I was busy on my own. So was Tuck. We don't know where Bo was. Probably on his way to the Cities."

"Early on he was at the dance. Like the rest of you. That's where he got into it with Cody for getting cozy with his girl, Sarah.''

"You're fulla shit," said Mac cheerfully. "Cody had his own woman—why'd he mess with another twitchy?''

" 'Cause he was always looking for something new, like the rest of us. And if you know Cody was with Winnie, you must've been around.''

"Sure, early on, like you said. Later I got me a girl and left.''

"Who was the girl?''

"None of your goddamned business.''

"You'd be surprised how far my business goes.''

He smiled, reached down, straightened up, and moved around the bar's end. I slipped off my stool as Tucker started his swing, ducked low enough to grip the stool leg, and caught him in the knees as he lunged forward. Mac tilted his head back trying to slip past his falling partner and stepped into my fist with his Adam's apple. The billy club fell from his fist and he sat down with his eyes popping and both hands at his throat.

I set up the fallen stool, pulled Tucker into a sitting position with his back against the lower part of the bar, and crouched in front of Mac, who was still trying to breathe.

"It'll be fine in a day or two," I told him. "Then, when I've checked out a couple things, we'll talk some more. You get to know me, you'll like me. I'm part Irish myself."

From the look in his eyes I thought it might take a while to charm him, but I grinned anyway, patted him on the shoulder, and walked out leaving my beer undrunk. It only hurt a little.

8

I considered telling Purvis what had happened but doubted that he'd believe me, and it was equally doubtful that my partners in the waltz would be broadcasting it, so I went back to the car and told my story to Evangeline.

"Good Lord," she said, "you really know how to make friends, don't you?"

I said winning friends wasn't my target on this trip. The best I could hope for was a little respect. She said it was more likely I'd set myself up for a lynching.

"Fine. Maybe that'll bring old Bo back. From what I've heard, he wouldn't want to miss that kind of a party."

Evangeline dropped me off at the garage in Toqueville and I got Simpson, the owner, to take me back for a look at the Hendricksons' Dodge. He said every parent in town had tried to bring their kids around to see what came of speeding and booze.

It was an educational sight, but I ignored the smashed front end and looked over the rear bumper.

"You notice that?" I asked Simpson.

He stood by me and nodded glumly. "Rear bumper's all banged to hell."

"It didn't get that way from a head-on collision," I said.

He agreed.

I went over to talk with Al Jacobsen about it, but

before I could open my mouth he told me he was on his way to see Cody Jerome at the Aquatown hospital because the doc there said Cody was in shape to talk some. "Want to come along?"

I did, and we took off. I told him about the Dodge's rear end and what I'd heard about Cody's run-in with Bo Grummen in Cranston.

"Well," he said, "they sure didn't run the Dodge into that bank or there'd've been two cars piled up."

"Of course, but they could've rammed him enough to make the kid panic and cause the accident. What can we do about getting Bo back in town?"

"That's Tom Purvis' job. Bo's from his town."

"The victims're in yours."

He didn't like that much and drove, glaring at the road.

"You could ask the Minneapolis police to check hotels. They could put a cop on a phone and find him."

He said he'd talk it over with Purvis.

After a few miles I asked if he knew Bo and his girl Sarah, and he nodded. "That Bo, he's one bad dude. One of those punks with a hard-on for the world. The kind of guy you pass a bottle and it comes back empty—if it comes back at all. Word's got it he's got friends because it's the only way to stay out of trouble with him."

I thought of the three guys back in Cranston and decided Bo must be a handful. None of them were exactly timid or frail.

"What about Sarah?" I asked.

He shrugged. "One of them cute flirty ones. Not awful bright. Boy-crazy since she was in pigtails." He turned his head and glanced at me. "You say you talked to Bo's buddies?"

I nodded.

"I'm surprised one of them didn't try to muss you up."

"I was careful," I assured him.

"You must've been—and lucky on top of it. Don't ever get two of 'em together. One at a time they're fairly reasonable. Get 'em together and whoosh!"

It was late afternoon when we got to the hospital, and a nurse told us Cody was in the examination room with a couple of doctors but would be out soon. We sat in the waiting room among bathrobed patients who were smoking and added our own clouds while thinking our own thoughts.

A doctor finally appeared, spotted Jacobsen, and fingered us down the hall to his office. We shook hands and he sat down behind a desk wearing his head mirror, stethoscope, and professional air. His thin face was all sharp angles and his brown eyes bored into us each time he looked up from his notes. He told us, in doctor talk, that the patient was severely shaken up, with a broken arm, a nose fracture, bruised ribs, and a fairly serious concussion.

"What I'm telling you," he concluded, "is that we have a man here who is badly disoriented and any testimony he offers may not be reliable."

"You telling me he's out of his head?" asked Jacobsen.

"No. But he is confused and depressed. His head hurts, he's nauseous, he's worried about his nose and how it's going to look, and we can't guarantee he'll recover full use of his left hand. And to be absolutely frank, I don't think it's advisable for him to see your partner here."

They both looked at my broken beak, and Jacobsen said okay, he'd go in alone and I'd wait in the hall.

So I waited and smoked and burned a little, too.

Eventually, Jacobsen came out looking tired, and we walked down the long halls, took an elevator to the main floor, and hiked to his car before he spoke.

"Cody says Kenny had a couple drinks before he ever saw the brothers at the dance. He swears he didn't give 'em anything and insists that Bo did. He also claims Sarah did the cozying up and did it so open Bo saw and called him out. Cody tried to talk his way out of it, couldn't, agreed to meet Bo after going to the can, and then ducked out. They was supposed to meet in the parking lot, where Cody's car was, so he dassn't go back there and he saw the Hendricksons on the street and asked for a ride. They agreed and went after Winnie for him, but one of the gang saw her with the boys and followed, and the next thing this big car was banging into the rear end of the Hendricksons' car as they drove along the highway. Kenny panicked, tried to lose them on a back road, hit the bend going too fast to turn, and wham!"

"Did they ever have a chance to really see the car?" I asked. "Could Cody convince anybody it was Bo's Graham Paige?"

"Probably not. It could've been Mac's car—he's got a big old Buick. Either way, Cody was probably looking back into headlights, so how could he be positive?"

We drove in silence a while. Al was grim-faced and glum. After a while I asked if he thought Cody was telling the truth all the way.

He sighed. "I think so, but who knows? Cody's been figuring angles all his life. If he thought he could shove the blame for this accident on somebody else, he'd do it.

That's how he's been. But in that bed today, he was a different guy. He's hurting and he's scared. He never asked me about anybody else in the car. I suppose he's been told and there's nothing else he wants to hear about it, but here's a guy never gave a damn for anybody but himself and now he's thinking and there ain't a thing he can think about that makes him feel good. That is one miserable son of a bitch. It's about enough to make a grown man cry."

He didn't shed any tears I could see, but he ran out of talk and gloomed all the rest of the way to Toqueville. Once in town he brightened up a little and when we pulled in front of City Hall he switched off the engine and twisted around in the seat to face me.

"How come Evangeline rode to Cranston with you?" he demanded.

"She didn't ride with me, I rode with her. She offered, I accepted."

"How come she offered?"

"I haven't got a working car right now."

He shook his head. "Something you'd ought to know without being told is, fellas in a town like this don't hate much of anything more than a stranger moving in and taking over a favorite girl. Now I know you're handy, but you ain't no Jack Dempsey and you can't whip every-body, and even if you could, I wouldn't want you banging our boys around. What you should do is tend to the business Judge Carlson hired you to handle and leave the goddamned romancing for when you get back to Corden or hit the road again."

Time was when I'd have told him where he could stick

that kind of advice, but I must be getting old because all I did was laugh.

"That's all right," he said. "You laugh all you want but pay me mind. I won't pertend I can throw you in jail for seeing Evie around, but the first time you get into a scrap with anybody at all it won't be that funny. You'll be in jail. These are my people and this is my town and you're just a fella with a temporary job, and a funny one at that. I sure as hell won't protect you. Now, you've already had your car wrecked—a lot worse could happen."

I told him I appreciated his problem and would take his friendly advice to heart. Then I asked if it was okay for me to eat at Doc Leigh's.

"You'd best skip that, too."

"I don't know. I can live without Evie, but giving up on Annabelle's cooking is going to be something else."

He frowned at me, straightened around in the seat, and said abruptly he had things to do. I got out and strolled back to Percy's Place.

The supper rush was easing off when I sat down at the counter and right after I'd ordered the roast beef dinner, Percy drifted over.

"Hear you went to Cranston," he said. "How'd it go?"

"Fine."

"I hear Evie's a good driver."

"I guess you hear about everything."

"Just about. She kind of goes for you, huh?"

"She hasn't proposed yet."

He grinned, sat down on the next stool, and leaned his elbow on the counter.

"You got the town pretty well stirred up, you know that?"

"How so?"

"Well, the town's split in two; half are for Brundage and two-thirds are for the judge. That don't add up, I know, but it's the kind of town we got. The ones that know which side the butter's on, they think they should be with Brundage, but nobody really likes him much so the sentiment's with the judge. That don't mean he's ahead, understand, but he gets the cheering."

"What's that got to do with me?"

"It's kinda complicated. See, the old-timers figure the accident was all Cody's fault and they'd like to see him nailed for it. Others figure the judge just wants to make Cody the goat because he's Brundage's fair-haired boy and it'd embarrass and burn him if you make it stick. And on top of all that, there's all these young bucks in town who don't like Cody but see you as the outside moving in on Arnie's girl, and while Arnie's not the most popular guy either, he's one of them and you ain't and Evie's the belle of the town and you're ringing her and they just naturally don't like that."

It sounded much like life in Corden.

"Well," I said, "my job's about finished, so you can just spread the word I won't be around much longer."

"You got the accident figured out?"

"I'll know in a day or two."

"Was it Cody's fault?"

"We'll see."

He grinned, straightened up, and called the waitress over to fill my coffee cup. Then he leaned toward me again. "You're slick, all right. Got it all doped out. You ever think about another little Toqueville problem?"

"Like what?"

"Ellsworth Ellison. The man who met the train."

"You mean, was it accidental or a suicide?"

"Or murder."

"Why'd anybody want to murder that poor bastard?"

He looked around the emptying café and gave me a solemn look. "Why'd Brundage hire him when he knew he was a boozer? What kind of a thing is that for a cold-blooded banker to do?"

"Maybe he wanted folks to think he was soft-hearted."

"They wouldn't have thought that if he'd adopted the man. No, come on now, don't you think that was a funny thing to do?"

It didn't make me laugh, but it did make me think some. After finishing dinner at Percy's I went around to Brundage's house.

9

I'd expected the woman who answered my knock to be a young maid or an aging wife, but what stood in front of me was a tall trim model in a green housedress that showed she had what she should in the right locations and nothing to spare. Her dark-gold hair swept back into a bun and there was a touch of silver around the temples.

"Yes?" she said, taking me in with cool gray eyes.

I told her my name and said I wanted to see Mr. Brundage.

She considered that a second or so, nodded, and went away. I gazed back at the yard, which was green, well trimmed, and lined with elms. They looked healthier than most around town and I guessed they'd been watered. Hollyhocks bloomed tall along the front porch, a little dusty-looking, yet bright.

The lady came back, opened the door, and led me through a big living room full of fat furniture, doilies, and fringed throws. The deep carpet's eight thousand shades of red reminded me of a slaughterhouse floor. I trailed the lady down a short hall beyond the living room and she waved me through a door to the right.

Brundage sat at a desk in a den hardly bigger than a walk-in closet. There was a high round window in the wall over the desk. A small lamp with a green shade lit the desktop, leaving the man's face in the shadows when he turned to peer at me. He looked mean, miserly, and interrupted.

"Well?"

"I don't think Cody was to blame for the accident."

He shoved his swivel chair back on its rollers and turned to face me. Suddenly he looked like the friendly banker.

"Really? Tell me about it."

I did and he liked it.

"Maud!" he yelled, "bring a chair in here."

He scowled impatiently when it didn't appear at once and, when she carried it in, told her to put it down and waved her out. She managed to act as if she were unaware of either one of us and stalked serenely off.

"That your wife?" I asked as I sat down.

"Never mind her, tell me about Cody. I know he's banged up, but how's he handling it?"

"The doc didn't want him to see me, so I only know what Jacobsen told me. He says Cody's down."

"The doc wouldn't let you in? Because of your broken nose?"

"I guess so."

He snorted. "A rare sensitivity. It'd probably do Cody good if he did wind up looking like you. Never slowed *you* down any, did it?"

"No, but mine wasn't pretty to begin with."

"Shouldn't make any difference to a real man. It wasn't looks got me where I am."

"You mean in Toqueville?"

He shot me a mean look. "You're quick on the needle, aren't you?"

"I like to keep even," I admitted.

He tilted his chair back and rested his small feet on the pedestal legs. "I'm not an easy man to like, but smart ones make the effort."

I didn't tell him I never made any claims to smart, I just decided to prove it.

"How come you hired a drunk as a bookkeeper?"

He didn't blink. "Ellsworth was the only male bookkeeper in town. And he'd work cheap. And it jolted hell out of the judge. Why'd you ask?"

"It struck me as funny. You hired him away from the judge?"

"I hired him after the judge fired him. How come you don't already know that?"

"I heard it. Just wanted your version."

He studied me a few seconds. "Okay, what're you fishing for? You already told the judge Cody wasn't to blame?"

"Not yet. This other question came up."

"I see. Evidently you don't think the judge'd pay you to investigate Ellsworth's death?"

When I didn't answer that he pulled a folded white handkerchief from his back pocket, examined it, wiped the corners of his dry mouth, and put it away.

"So what's Ellsworth to you?" he asked with a squint.

"I figured he might be something to you."

He grunted. "You think I'm going to hire another of the judge's castoffs, eh? You can maybe cash in on an old feud, that's what you're thinking. Why the hell should I hire you to investigate Ellsworth's death?"

"Because it might give you some advantage."

He stared for a moment, took a deep breath, and sighed. "All right. I *am* interested. What do you need?"

"I'd like the repair job on my car covered, and ten a day for expenses. Extra if I have to make a trip."

"Jeez! You've got more crust than my wife's deep-dish pie. You make any trips, we talk it over first. But before we make any deal, you finish with the judge. I don't want any accusations that I've bought you off."

I said fine and left.

10

Annabelle was sitting on her front porch with Alma in her lap when I got to her house. Alma squirmed free, hopped to the floor, and ran down the steps to meet me. I picked her up and got a great hug.

"You missed supper," Annabelle said ominously.

"I was warned off."

She drew up, scowling. "What do you mean?"

"The town law thinks I'm gonna disturb the peace if I get too cozy with your family."

Her face went from a scowl to surprise, then skepticism and annoyance. "That," she said, "from a man like you, is a ridiculous excuse. Are you trying to convince me a few words from Al Jacobsen scared you?"

"No, but he made me think a little. You mind if I smoke out here?"

"I don't care if you burn."

I did a little, but after a few seconds sat down on the step, parked Alma beside me, and rolled a smoke. She watched and stuck out her tongue when I started to lick the paper. I let her do it and then she folded her arms and tucked them between her knees.

"You're real helpful," I told her. "You been doing anything for Annabelle?"

She shook her head.

"I hope you haven't been talking her to death."

She didn't think that was worth comment but smiled a little.

"Careful," I warned her, "you do that too much and your face might crack."

She ducked her blond head and, when I patted it, leaned into my side.

Next door the screen slammed and I looked up to see Evangeline crossing the lawn. Annabelle came down from the porch and we all sat in a row on the step.

"What'd you learn from Cody?" asked Evangeline.

I described the non-interview and what Jacobsen had told me.

Annabelle, looking upset, said, "Did Al believe all that garbage?"

"Seems like."

"Do you?" asked Evangeline.

"Yeah. It was just about what I figured. I checked the back bumper of the Dodge. It's banged up real good."

Neither of the women said anything about how the judge would react to all that but they were both thinking about it. Finally, Annabelle asked when I was going to report to the judge.

I looked at Evangeline and asked, "How about now?"

"Let's put Alma to bed first."

So I carried Alma upstairs and told her a story about a dam collapse I watched once. It was an earth dam that simply slipped away while I was standing on the observation tower off to the side. There wasn't a sound— I couldn't even hear the workmen yell or their boots strike the ground as they fled from the collapsing support. I told her they all got away, but they didn't. The disintegration caught up with a guy in high boots who kept looking back, and I saw his clutching hands disappear under the roiling water and come up once and then disappear forever. It was like watching ants. It's hard to feel involved when the tragedy's far away and you don't know what the guy looked like, let alone how he treated folks he knew.

I wished I knew more about Kenny Hendrickson and his brother Don. And even the wise guy, Cody, who, for all I knew, had done more for Alma than I had but had only won her dislike. And I wished most of all I could've known Winnie, who'd been so wild, independent, and crazy about her kid.

When I rose to leave, Alma murmured something too low to hear but didn't wake.

Evangeline walked across the lawn with me to see her uncle. He was sitting in a big easy chair under a fringed floor lamp in the far corner of a comfortable-sized living room. Open windows flanked him and the curtains moved easy in the cross draft. Crickets sang outside. The judge was wearing an open-collared white shirt, and that with the white hair and pale face made him look ghostly in the shadowed room. He peered at me through the top third of his trifocals and frowned. I had the sudden silly notion that he thought I'd come in to ask for the hand of his niece. At any rate, that's how welcoming his gaze was.

He lowered a leather bound book to his lap and straightened up. "Good evening."

"He's got a report for you," said Evangeline. Her tone let him know he wouldn't like it.

The judge's face assumed a sociable expression, he invited me to sit down and when I did, Evangeline plopped on the couch beside me.

I described Cody's story. The judge nodded a couple

times and when I was through asked if I had any witnesses.

"There's nobody but Alma, and she hasn't had a whole lot to say. But everything I've picked up about everybody involved makes me think it more than likely Bo and his gang were the bad guys. Now Bo's left town and nobody knows for sure where he is. I've checked the Dodge's rear bumper and it's all banged to hell and it sure didn't get that way from a head-on collision. If you want to spend the money, I'll keep poking, but I'm not going to come up with anything you want to know."

He scowled, thought some, tipped his head back, and said all right, how much did he owe me? I told him three days' worth. He got up with some puffing and grunting and went down the hall.

I looked at Evangeline, who said, "You haven't exactly given him much satisfaction."

"He wanted satisfaction, he should've hired me to paint a sign."

She grinned sadly, crossed her legs under her skirt, and folded her hands across her knees. "I suppose this means you'll be moving on."

"Pretty soon. Will Annabelle take on Alma?"

"I'm not sure. Maybe. She's not awfully eager. She had two miscarriages, you know. She's afraid of getting hurt again."

I didn't see much sense in that since obviously she couldn't miscarry this one, but I kept quiet.

The judge came back and handed me a check. I folded it and stuck it behind the tobacco pouch in my shirt pocket. The judge looked older and Evangeline seemed so forlorn I began to feel like a turd about working for

Brundage. The hell with it, I decided, I'll cut out clean in the morning and head for Sioux Falls.

Evangeline walked to the street with me. A car engine started half a block to the east. Evangeline slipped her arm through mine.

"I'm going to miss you," she said. "You're a very interesting, different kind of bum. It's too bad you're not taller."

"And golden-haired? Yeah, well, it'd be nice if you were a little smarter, but what the hell."

She started to jerk her arm free, but I gripped her wrist and grinned at her.

She laughed. "All right, we're even. Now let go. I'll see you tomorrow."

We were in the middle of the block when we parted, just a ways from the hotel. If the car hadn't been still easing closer I'd have tried to kiss her, but it distracted me and she moved off.

I walked toward the corner. The car speeded up, pulled past, and stopped with a squeal of rubber. Both doors popped open and two men scrambled out. The manly form of Arnie was recognizable at once; his husky partner was a stranger. They barred my path and the partner spoke in a voice thick with rage.

"This here's a farewell party, asshole. You're through. We don't need any goddamned old cons messing with our girls."

I reached for my fixings as I shook my head. "Can't go. Somebody messed up my car."

"You can take a bus, a train, or walk—we don't care which. But you're going tonight, on your feet or on your back."

I opened my tobacco sack and started filling my cigarette paper. "What's your name, buster?" I asked.

"Duke Peterson—and don't you ever forget it."

"I'll call you Swede."

He must've been Norsk because that made him start a haymaker. I pitched the tobacco in his eyes and, when his hands flew up, hooked him in the gut. Low. As he folded, Arnie jumped for me. I grabbed his brawny arm, did a swing-around, and threw him over my shoulder and halfway across the street. Duke started up and I caught him right between the eyes with my knee. He went down on his back. I picked up my tobacco sack and strolled into the hotel.

Inside I puffed a little and took what satisfaction I could in the fact that big men are easy to surprise when they take on a small one. The next round wouldn't be so easy.

The old man at the registration counter looked some surprised when I told him I was staying another week and paid in advance. I guessed he knew what was supposed to have happened out front, but after his first reaction he only nodded and put the money in the cash register.

While getting ready for bed I tried to think of a sensible reason why I'd changed my plans about leaving town. I decided the only defensible explanation was that I wanted to make sure about Alma's future before I left.

11

"I hear you're leaving town," said Percy as he joined me at his counter the next morning while I was eating breakfast.

"Not me. I may buy a house and settle down."

He grinned. "Go on, you didn't get paid enough to buy a house, not even here."

"Yeah, but my credit's good, right?"

He grinned some more and asked was I going to the funeral in the afternoon. I admitted I hadn't thought about it.

"Gonna be the biggest we ever had. One ceremony for the three of 'em. That was old man Hendrickson's idea. He probably figured it'd go over big with the judge."

"He got a case coming up?"

"Not that I know of, but Hendrickson's a man who thinks ahead. And speaking of that, you going to adopt Alma?"

"I don't know. Would that give me a leg up on the local social ladder?"

"Oh, hell yes. Then all you'd have to do is marry Evangeline and get a steady job."

I shook my head. "Percy, you're something. I've had people try to run me out of town lots of ways but you're the first that ever threatened me with a ball and chain."

He was so tickled by that he could hardly stay on his stool, and when he got his breath he suggested I go

91

across the street to old Jake Haskell at the grocery store.
He'd said he liked what I did for Percy and would like me
to do his windows.

Percy moved off to talk with somebody important
while I wondered if I could get away with sign painting
on Brundage's time. I was just finishing my coffee when
Arnie slipped through the front door, looked around
sheepishly, and came over to climb on the stool Percy had
left.

"Last night wasn't my idea," he told me.

"It didn't seem like your style."

"It's just that Duke's a real old friend and he's awfully
hot-headed—"

"He's not fast enough to be hot-headed and healthy.
He could wind up punchy."

Arnie didn't want to talk about his friend. "I heard
you're leaving town anyway."

"I was. Changed my mind. Besides, I've got a new
job."

He looked wise and leaned on the counter. "Going to
work for Brundage?"

That startled me and I was glad the waitress came by to
offer coffee. I accepted it, thanked her, and waited till she
walked away.

"Why," I said, "would you get the notion the
banker'd want to hire me?"

He stared at me for a moment, then glanced in the
mirror and turned back to me. "I think you're an
opportunist. You figured out Brundage would pay more
to keep Cody clear than the judge would to prove he was
at fault."

"That's a neat notion. But the facts are, I found Cody

wasn't to blame and that part's settled and the judge has paid me off."

He considered that a moment, then hunched his shoulders. "So Brundage hired you for something else."

"Like what?"

"He wants you to find out what happened to Ellsworth. That's it, isn't it?"

"What'd that gain him?"

"I don't know." He sat back and dropped his hands in his lap. "It's just the only real mystery around this town. There's got to be a reason why Brundage hired a notorious drunk in the first place. I don't believe for a second he all of a sudden turned solicitous about the down-and-out, any more than I believe Ellsworth just walked into the side of a train. It doesn't make sense, not any of it."

"Okay. Make my job easy. What happened?"

He slumped and looked glum. "I don't know. There's something involving corruption and money, you can bet on that. I can't imagine what Ellsworth could know that'd be useful to Brundage, but there must be something."

"Like maybe the judge took a few bribes?"

"No, not that . . ." He looked up nervously and took in the room through the mirror. "But there could be lots of things. It might even be his brother did something— they were partners, you know. In a town like this everybody's involved in everybody's business and there can be strange entanglements."

"So bad it could get a man murdered?"

"Well, certainly not by the judge. But he's not above using people or exploiting the law. I've seen him manipulate people, use the passions at hand, if you know what I mean."

"I think I can figure that out. Who's the judge know that'd get that excited about Ellsworth?"

"Well, there's Cody, except he's not the type. He'd get somebody else to do the dirty work. And there was Winnie. She was tired of him and she was awfully impulsive."

"You do complicate a problem."

"Yes," he confessed sadly.

"Ever hear about how Cody treated Alma?"

"No. She must've been a nuisance to him, but now that you mention it, I guess he'd never dare let Winnie think so. She was a tigress about Alma. When they were at a movie once, a guy got nasty because Alma started fussing—she was just a baby then—and this man hollered, 'Shut that brat up,' and Winnie hauled off and hit him with her purse and about put his eye out. She'd have been in trouble if the judge hadn't defended her."

"Who was the guy?"

"Some Norwegian farmer. I don't think he ever came back to town."

When the waitress came around Arnie ordered coffee and hunched over it, frowning.

"Did you ever hear," I asked, lowering my voice, "that the judge was a little sweet on Winnie?"

He looked shocked, shook his head, and pulled his elbows off the counter. "No, of course not. Why, she was almost young enough to be his granddaughter."

"Uh-huh. And her husband worked for the judge. Was she around his office or house in those days?"

Arnie didn't know or wouldn't say. The whole idea offended him, but I could see it worried him, too. I suppose I should feel guilty about putting nasty suspicions in such an innocent mind. After a while I gave up on him, paid my bill, and left.

There were no loitering cars or hostile youths in the bright street as I hiked toward the Leighs'.

Annabelle let me in and led the way to the kitchen. I sat down beside the doc, who was indulging in a late breakfast after having delivered a baby on a farm in the wee hours. Evangeline drifted in and sat across from me.

"I thought you were leaving town," she said. She acted as if we had not agreed we'd see each other again and had parted on good terms. Perhaps she'd heard that I'd paid for another week at the hotel.

"I got talked into sticking around," I said.

Doc Leigh side-eyed me and almost grinned but managed to squelch it. "Report has it," he said, "that a couple local boys tried to convince him he should leave town last night. Evidently they weren't very convincing."

"Where'd you hear that?"

"Emma," guessed Evangeline, "the all-knowing telephone operator."

"True," said Doc, wiping his mouth with his napkin.

Annabelle offered me a fresh doughnut, giving me a choice of powdered or plain. I took the powdered and licked my fingers between bites. It was a tad south of tough and about the best I ever ate. I told her so, and she brought out a smile like a sunbeam after a shower.

Alma wandered in all sleepy-eyed, piped me, and trotted over to throw her arms across my lap. "Hi, Uncle Carl," she said.

It was the first time she'd volunteered more than a word to me, so I picked her up and rewarded her with the last bite of my doughnut. She said thank you so formally everyone laughed except the doc. He studied her like she was something in a specimen bottle. For some reason I tried to imagine him in bed with Annabelle, but I couldn't picture it as normal. I figured he'd have to examine her privates with a tongue depresser before he tried to make an entry.

I took Alma along as I walked toward his office with the doc and asked if he'd checked up on Cody Jerome. He said yes, there had been progress. Cody's depression had lifted some and he was eating almost normally but he still avoided talking about the accident. He hadn't asked anything about Winnie once he learned she was dead and had shown no reaction to news that the daughter had survived.

"You think the cops believe his story about Bo and his gang causing the accident?"

"I don't know. But unless there's another witness besides Cody, it's not likely anything'll happen even if they accept his version."

"Is Purvis afraid of those guys?"

"Maybe a little. I don't think he's a physical coward, but he doesn't deal well with complications. He wants everything cut-and-dried."

"You know this Bo Grummen at all?"

"I know a little about what he's like. Back when he was playing football for Cranston, they had a game here and he got two fingers broken. I set and bandaged them and he paid me no more mind than as if I were squeezing a pimple. All he could think about was getting back in that game and hitting the boy who stepped on his hand. I don't think he'd have noticed if I amputated both fingers. And, I should add, he did hit the other fellow hard enough to crack two ribs. He was a formidable boy; I suspect he is a dangerous man."

Alma and I left the doc at his office and went back to the park where we'd watched the boys play ball. Now the area was deserted except for a couple sparrows pecking in the dust. A squirrel raced out on an elm branch over us, paused to twitch his tail, and scolded us. I mimicked his chatter and Alma laughed and tried it too. She was very disappointed when the squirrel dashed off.

We wandered back toward the Leighs' but as we were passing the judge's house next door, Alma tugged on my hand and pulled me toward the front door. I assumed she wanted to visit the man, but she tugged me around on the walk to the back and to the swing beside a sandbox in the yard. I lifted her onto the swing seat and pushed her for a little while. She kept looking toward the house as if she expected to see her mother look through the window or come to the door.

Her face suddenly turned anxious, and I looked toward the back entrance and saw the inner door open. The next moment the judge was standing there, watching us through the screen.

When I looked at Alma her face was blank.

The judge pushed the screen door open and came to join us, wearing a smile that didn't quite fit. Alma acknowledged his greeting with a solemn nod while she sat with her arms around the ropes and her small hands clasped together across her chest.

"How does it happen," said the judge, still watching her but addressing me, "that you're still in town?"

"Doing a job for Mr. Brundage."

His head jerked and his eyes narrowed. "Painting?"

"Investigation."

"Of what?"

"Ellsworth's death."

He took a deep breath while watching the gently swinging child and glanced at me again. "Is this investigation *your* idea?"

"You might call it mutual."

He looked past me across the yard and nodded thoughtfully. "You're also interested in Evangeline, aren't you?"

"I don't think she was involved."

"I'd hardly suggest that. What I think is, you wanted to stay in town and you're opportunistic enough to figure a way of getting paid while you pay court, in your own quaint way, to my niece."

I gave him my harmless smile and admitted the lady did interest me. "But," I went on, "this business with Ellsworth bothers me like a flea in a bedroll. There's got to be a reason why both you guys hired that boozer, and it wasn't Christian love. And just as interesting is you bringing Winnie into your house to take care of you. That's pretty different, you know? Taking in a mother with a kid that young, and a woman with quite a reputation for things besides housekeeping talents at that."

He stared at me, twitched, and turned toward the house. "I can't take this sun—we'll go inside."

Alma surrendered the swing reluctantly and hung on to my hand as we went into the house and through a hall to the dark living room with its drawn shades. It was wonderfully cool and restful. The judge gave Alma a small glass of cold water and poured iced tea for us from a pitcher he got out of the icebox.

"I brought Winnie and Alma into my house, believe it or not, out of compassion. Just as I first hired Ellsworth. I'll admit I couldn't stand living alone after my wife died—I felt a great need for company and house help. People who live in this town and know me understood that perfectly. As far as I know, there was never any gossip until Ellsworth's death and then certain elements blamed me for separating the couple, but the responsible citizens knew perfectly well that marriage was a farce and gave me credit for helping Winnie out."

"How was her housekeeping?"

He smiled a little ruefully. "Better than I expected in some ways, worse in others. She could be a good cook when she was in the mood but her housekeeping was slapdash. Never learned to make a bed decently and always left dust rags around or few dishes unwashed. She made fine coffee and tea. Strong. Evangeline's never learned you must make tea strong if you're going to ice it."

"How's *her* cooking?"

"Evangeline's? Adequate." He said it as if he were fearful of lauding his niece's qualifications as a mate. It struck me funny he'd worry about that when obviously he figured I only planned to bed the girl and then desert her.

I asked what Winnie's parents had been like.

"Very interesting. Amos Anderson was her father. I never saw him in his prime—he was ill when they came here but still, at times, vigorous and forceful. A constant talker, up to the minute on politics, business, and anything you care to mention. Had a suspiciously broad knowledge of fraud laws. I guessed early on he'd been a confidence man. Obviously had an excellent education, made a lot of money, and traveled broadly."

"Why'd he come here?"

"He claimed it was to be near some cousins, but I suspect it was to hide."

"He talk about himself?"

"Never about his vocation. Did you know that Ellsworth came to town with him? Ellsworth was one of his favorite topics. According to Amos, Ellsworth had been a child prodigy. Went to Harvard about the age your average kid enters primary school. Got written up in the *Times*. Phenomenal child, mathematical and language genius. He graduated with honors at a ridiculous age, was expected to get a doctorate and have a splendid career. But he dropped out of graduate school early on, left his parents, and took to the bottle. Amos met him in a bar out East, hired him right off the stool, so to speak, and brought him back here. I asked Amos if the boy'd been so wonderful, why'd he given up all that promise, and he said the boy got sick of being treated like a freak and used like a guinea pig. According to Amos, the only way to get along with this genius was to treat him like an ordinary person. I followed that advice, although at times it wasn't easy, when I hired him after Amos died. It worked fine until I got worried about his heavy drinking and told him he should cut down. He quit me that afternoon and was working for Brundage the next week. He was a self-destructive man. It was no surprise to me when he killed himself. That was just the next logical step in his basically illogical life."

"You think maybe Winnie's moving out and taking Alma was the last straw?"

"Not for a minute. He didn't care a rap for either of

them or anyone or any*thing* else. Never showed a hint of interest in his wife's affair with Cody. Wouldn't surprise me if their marriage was never consummated.''

We both looked at Alma, who was dozing in my lap. The judge shook his head. ''She's no proof to the contrary.''

''You said Winnie's old man had money. What happened to it?''

''He squandered a good deal of it on that big house he built and left the rest to his wife, but she was at least half mad and went through most of it by the time she died. They were all mad in that crowd except Winnie. She was different, but not crazy.''

''Tell me about her mother.''

''Sophia? She was *some*thing. While Amos lived she kept in the background. I assumed she was one of those types that hang on strong men. The type that'd accept suttee.'' He shook his head. ''I'll tell you, when he died, she bloomed. Became a suffragette. Old Amos wasn't cool in his grave when she took to the street and the stump. More energy than Satan and about as much self-restraint. I was her lawyer and had to get her out of jail three different times.''

''She lived here?''

''No, their house was in Cranston. It wasn't clear, of course, and eventually she sold her rights for a song. Too busy gallivanting to meetings and demonstrations to pay any mind to money. Said the Lord would provide. The most he provided her was energy, and that in abundance. Didn't have a particle of common sense, but oh, how she had the words and the message!''

''How'd the daughter come to marry Ellsworth?''

''Probably because she got sick of her mother. And Ellsworth was around while she was growing up, so she saw how much smarter he was than anybody else she ever met. She probably saw him as a tragic, romantic soul and dreamed of reforming him, making him realize his promise. It didn't take her long to find out that was all nonsense."

"You talk to her much when she came to work for you?"

"No, I'm afraid not. I tried a little at first, but she soon made it clear she'd not stand for living with any Dutch uncle. We reached an understanding early on. She wasn't to do any carrying on in my house and I'd mind my own business about what she did outside of it as long as she didn't become notorious."

"I heard a rumor she might be an heiress."

He scowled. "I suppose Brundage gave you that."

"What's the difference who told me? Was she?"

"Well, if it was Brundage, you should know he was just trying to stir up something against me. Take anything that man says with a shaker of salt. Now I just told you, her father left some money but the mother went through it."

"You sure he wasn't smart enough to guess she'd do a thing like that and maybe leave some money in a trust or something?"

"You didn't think of that yourself. That's another Brundage idea. Typical of the man."

"I get lots of notions myself," I told him. "Like I even wonder if maybe Winnie wasn't something more than a maid to you."

He fooled me and, instead of getting mad, laughed. "You'd never think anything like that," he told me, "if you'd known the girl. She went for young men. A man my age wouldn't interest her a second."

"A man your age, with money and power, he can interest any woman."

"That's fatuous. A man like you can interest a woman. What the devil does that prove?"

"I guess it proves it never pays to argue with a lawyer."

I thought about trying to roll a cigarette with Alma in my lap but decided, considering where the dialogue had gone, I'd rather avoid waking her and gave it up.

"What'd Winnie's ma look like?" I asked.

"A bony woman. All chin and elbows. Amos married her when she was a kid, dominated her long as he lived. Once he was gone, she was determined never to be bossed again. I wasn't fool enough to try."

I shifted Alma slightly and she promptly woke and yawned. It seemed like time to leave, but as I put Alma on her feet, Evangeline stalked in. She wore a trim navy-blue dress with a white collar and looked young enough to be fresh from high school. She glanced at the judge and then turned to glare at me.

"Uncle Cal, do you know who this man is working for now?"

"He told me. Brundage. So what's the word around town? What're they saying he's to do?"

"Find something against you."

The judge leaned back in his chair and smiled easy. "Does that worry you? You think he can do it?"

That jolted her some and she opened her mouth, closed it, and sat down on the sofa. "Well," she said, "doesn't it bother you—the disloyalty?"

"You don't hire loyalty," he said, looking at me. "It's supposed to gain allegiance when you pay a man, but Carl doesn't work for me anymore. Do people think I nudged Ellsworth into that train? Is that what Brundage thinks?'' he asked me.

"The only time he mentioned you," I said, "was when he said I was to be sure you and I were finished before I did any work for him. He didn't want to be accused of hiring away another of your employees."

"Interesting. A point delicate enough for a lawyer to consider. I've often thought Brundage missed his calling. How does it happen you didn't try to persuade me to pay you for investigating Ellsworth's death?"

"You never seemed that interested."

Alma walked over to the window, and the three of us watched. The sun came through the lace curtains and made her blond hair glow. After a moment she turned, met our collective stare, and smiled shyly.

Evangeline said the poor child must be bored to death by us and the judge suggested she take her back out to the swings for a little while. Evangeline, to my surprise, accepted that, took Alma's hand, and set off. Alma threw me an anxious look but went along passively.

The judge propped his right ankle on his left knee and gave me a judicial gaze. "I'd guess," he said, "that you actually believe Brundage hired Ellsworth just to find out what he could about my business. Try to find some scandal about me and Winnie, or my involvement with the family. Something, anything, damaging. Right?"

"It seems likely, yeah."

He sighed, put both feet flat on the floor, and leaned back. "Well, sir, the simple fact is, no matter where or who you snoop around, I never tried to hire Ellsworth back, never spoke to him about anything confidential, never had reason to be concerned about anything he ever learned about my professional ethics or financial integrity. And even if he *had* learned anything awful I'd done, he was the last man on earth to exploit it."

He said that with an edge of contempt but his expression was all tolerance. I was reminded of the kid who met the barking dog that wagged its tail and asked, "Which end do you believe?"

12

The funeral for Winnie and the Hendrickson brothers pulled in almost as big a crowd as a Fourth of July celebration. The Presbyterian Church was packed to the gunwales, with people standing in the back clear out to and down the steps in front. There had been some grumbling about Winnie being ceremonied in a church she had never belonged to but the judge prevailed and generally folks approved because of course it made a better show with all three victims in one package.

I hadn't planned to get involved, but when Alma turned fussy Evangeline ran me down and insisted I had to come along and comfort the child. There was something of a scramble to find a suit for me and I never learned where they found the one I ended up in. It was tight across the shoulders and free in the middle but the sleeves were fair and Doc Leigh loaned me a tie that the funeral director tied for me. Contrary to stories told, he didn't have me lie down so he could do it.

I was never certain Alma really knew what was going on. She solemnly clung to my hand and, like the day when I pulled her out of the car, always seemed on the edge of coming unglued. At the same time she drew back and I felt if nothing nudged her wrong, she could sail right over it all.

The minister had a lot to say about the Hendrickson brothers and the tragedy for their family. I doubt either boy would've recognized the paragons described in the elegy, but it made the parents miserably proud and that was his job. He skipped over Winnie with a light touch, saying she was a free spirit, well-meaning, a loving mother, and doubtless forgiven by Jesus and accepted above, where she would be reunited with her misguided husband who'd gone before to prepare a place.

It all made a body wonder why most of us stayed in the world to fight adversity and evil.

People crowded in so hard after the service I had to pick up Alma to keep her from getting trampled. At first she looked at the faces, wide-eyed and sober, then she turned away, pushed her head against my chest, and just hung on. People patted her gently and I got a few touches and a lot of murmured blessings and the judge held my elbow and steered me to his car and we got in and people cleared away from the front. We moved off with them standing around waving, weeping, and gawking.

Early that night I took her up to her room and she asked me to tell her a story about a prince.

I said I'd never known any princes.

"Pertend," she said.

I asked if she'd ever heard about Cinderella. She shook her head. So I told it as well as I could remember, and she was quiet for a little while and then asked if Cinderella had blond hair.

I said sure.

"Did she die?"

"In fairy tales, nobody dies but the dragon."

She said that was nice and went to sleep.

13

It was still early evening when I entered the beer parlor, and before I'd downed two glasses I knew the owner's name was Miller and he'd been in business since prohibition ended and a couple former bootleggers set him up. He didn't say whether they got a cut or supplied him with stock, and I didn't ask. What counted for him was that in his place he could talk about sports and women eighteen hours a day and that's all he wanted in this world.

Yeah, he'd served Ellsworth his last drinks. Nope, the man hadn't been any drunker that night than usual, although the fact was, usual was more drunk than most when you talked about Ellsworth.

"What'd he talk about?"

"Mostly he said, 'Gimme another.' "

"Ever mention his family?"

"Nope."

"Guys ever get on him?"

"Nah. He kept to himself and nobody noticed him much. Now and then some wise guy'd try to get a rise out of him by asking how he got along with Cody or stuff like that. He'd say fine and grin. Couldn't get a rise out of that fella with a hotfoot."

I kept pushing and he finally admitted one of the regulars talked with Ellsworth quite a bit. When I asked for the guy's name Miller got annoyed and said he couldn't remember every mouth in the joint, but as soon as he remembered the name it was clear he prided himself on just that. The guy's name was Odie Frye. I got his address and left.

Odie Frye told me he'd worked thirty years for the gas company and was celebrating his third year of retirement. He was small, bald, and cheerful as a Halloween pumpkin. His small bungalow overlooked the north edge of town and gave him a dandy view of prairie interrupted by nothing but fenceposts and telephone poles a quarter of a mile away.

I sat on a wicker chair out on his little porch while he swung creakily on a white high-backed bench hung from the porch ceiling.

"You think Ellsworth killed himself?" I asked.

"Who knows? Ellsworth was a very special kind of man. Take his name. How many people you talked to about him?"

"Maybe half a dozen."

"Uh-huh. All called him Ellsworth, didn't they? No Elly, or Al, or even Ellison, except ones didn't really know him. 'Course nobody *really* knew him, not even me. He was a genius, you know that? Got written up by newspapers in the big city back East when he was no more than a tad. Talked all kinds of languages, was a wizard with figures, had a fancy degree, and with all that he wound up a bookkeeper in Toqueville. Don't get me wrong, this is a nice enough town, but here was a man could've lived any place he wanted in the whole world probably, and he wound up here. Keeping books. Know what he told me? He said figures were all that counted. They didn't lie. And then he grinned at me and said, but liars can figure. You know he never used an adding machine? He could go down a page of figures, didn't matter how big or long, add 'em and never miss."

"He tell you that?"

"Nah, he never bragged. I heard it from people who worked for the judge and one fella who'd known Winnie's pa, the fella that brought him here. I asked Ellsworth once was he really as good as they said and he shrugged me off."

"He ever talk about his bosses?"

"He didn't ever really talk about anything. I'd ask, sometimes he'd answer, sometimes he wouldn't, and when he did answer it was with a question. I didn't mind but it drove other guys nuts."

"You always answered his questions, huh?"

"I tried. I'm a sociable man. Say what I think and give the other fella a chance to do likewise. I understood Ellsworth. I don't mean the man, if you get me, I mean the way he was. See, his problem was, he was so smart there wasn't anybody he could talk to."

"Why didn't he stay home and talk to his wife?"

"Oh well, a man doesn't get anywhere talking to a wife. All they care about is kids, clothes, and if he's lucky, food. And if he's unlucky, money. That's where trouble starts."

"You think he got so lonely he just walked into a train to end it all?"

He shook his head. "He might, or he mightn't. You come right down to cases, I'd say no. Ellsworth was perfectly happy drinking himself to death and he wasn't in any particular hurry. He never cried in his booze about losing his wife or kid, and he didn't complain about his

job or the boss like most fellas. He just worked his days
and drank his nights."

"Did he get blind drunk?"

"Just good and sozzled. Matter of fact, that last night
he was feeling better than usual, I thought. I asked him
how it went and he said just jim-dandy. Mostly when I
asked him that he said they were just going. So I asked
him had he got a raise and he said he didn't need one."

Odie stopped the bench's swinging, stood up, and
moved to the porch railing a moment to stare out across
the billowing field of bleached wheat.

"I thought lots about him when I heard he was dead.
He was the kind of fella might think of killing himself as
a kind of joke on us all. He'd get a kick out of shocking
folks."

"You ever find out which of his bosses he liked
working for best?"

He turned and grinned at me. "Now that's real funny
you'd ask that, because it's just the question I put to him
once and what he said was, 'If you must work for a
crook, it's better to have one who's open about it instead
of closed.' I thought about that and I figured since lots of
people think Mr. Brundage is at least tricky, and most
folks see the judge as part saint, that he was saying
Brundage was the best. But then I remembered he
worked for that fella Amos Anderson and some say he
was a con man—so I don't know. That's the way
Ellsworth talked. Riddles."

I asked if he was familiar with Bo Grummen, of
Cranston, and his friends. He was, or at least to the
extent that he'd taken in all the gossip about the night of
the accident and the reports of Bo's involvement and later
trip to the Cities to get married.

"Funny thing," he told me, as he climbed back on the bench swing, "from what I hear, that Sarah gal was the girlfriend of Bo's buddy up until that night."

He didn't know which one.

I thanked him for talking with me and said he was quite a thinker. He admitted that was true. We shook hands and I left.

14

Since it seemed likely Annabelle would be as hostile as Evangeline about my new job, I thought things over a while the next day before deciding to risk going back for lunch. Since caution never had got me anywhere, I headed for the house.

It was hotter than usual that noon and when I came up the walk there was Alma, standing behind the screen door with her nose pressed against the lower panel. She shoved the door open and ran to meet me.

I picked her up and told her she was looking good and she put her finger in the dimple on my chin and wanted to know why I had a hole there. I told her it was a dent, not a hole, and before I could expand on that Annabelle showed up and told us to get on in before we both got sunstroke. A moment later we were in the kitchen eating egg salad sandwiches and drinking iced tea. I'm about as crazy for egg salad as I am for porridge, but she used lots of mustard in hers and after I added a little salt and pepper it wasn't too bad. She also came up with some great dill pickles.

"Evangeline's furious with you," said Annabelle with more than polite satisfaction. "She says you sold out."

"Why should she be sore? The judge isn't."

"Don't be too sure. Just because he didn't throw a conniption fit doesn't mean he's not sore."

"I did what he hired me to do. If he's not satisfied with the facts, that's his problem."

"Well, you can hardly expect him to be tickled pink with what you call 'facts' when they got you a new job working for a man he hates."

"So how come you're tolerating me?"

"I'm not sure I am. I guess it's sort of like watching a strange animal in your yard. You think it may be trouble, but you can't help watching to see what the critter'll do before you try to chase it off or get somebody to shoot it."

I looked at Alma, who was taking all this in, and asked if she thought I was some kind of strange animal. She grinned shyly, shook her head, and looked down in her lap.

After lunch I took her over to the judge's yard and pushed her a while on the swing. Then I asked if she remembered anything about the night of the car wreck.

She shook her head.

"You like Annabelle," I asked.

She nodded.

"How about the judge?"

She got a neutral expression.

"Did your ma like him?"

She shrugged.

I told her that all women were hard to understand but she was probably going to set new world records, and if her face hadn't been so innocent I'd have sworn it got a smug look.

I walked her down to the soda parlor, bought her an ice cream cone, and then went over to City Hall, where we found Al sitting at his desk chewing on a pencil.

"What do you hear about Cody Jerome?" I asked.

"He's not pinching nurses yet, but I hear he's coming along."

"You figure he could survive the sight of me?"

He considered me soberly and said I could give it a try. He said that carefully enough for me to guess he'd been talking with the judge and I'd lost ground. I asked him about bus schedules to Aquatown and he said there'd been one at twelve noon and would be another tomorrow, same time.

I went to see Percy and after some chatter he arranged for me to ride with a customer who was picking up some tools there for the hardware store in Toqueville. He'd be coming back by supper time.

The driver had a Finnish name I never got straight and he had nothing to say after he remarked that Alma was sure a cutey. I got her to hum "Row, Row, Row Your Boat" with me after the first ten miles and by the time we reached Aquatown's city limits she was even singing the words. She caught the rhythm right off.

It took us a while to get into Cody's room, but we made it because Alma charmed the socks off the nurses and the one doctor I met. He was different from the first guy, who'd been sure I'd scare his patient to death.

Cody did a double-take when we entered the room but acted pleased to see us. I think he was so bored he'd have welcomed the four plug-uglies who'd put him there. "Hey!" he told Alma, "you're looking great!"

She didn't show any great enthusiasm about the greeting but didn't hang back when I pulled up a chair beside the bed and sat with her in my lap.

I told him who I was, and he said yeah, he guessed that the minute I came in. Al had told him about me.

"How you making out with Evie?" he asked.

"The romance is in eclipse. She thinks I've sold her uncle out."

"Just like a woman, always expect the worst of us." He grinned. "Of course they're usually right. Did you?"

"No."

"Well, you sure's hell helped me and girly here, so by God, you got yourself a friend for life. I never forget a favor. You want one from me, you got it."

"Okay. Tell me about Bo."

He shook his head solemnly. "There, my friend, is a hard case. Now anybody around town'll tell you, Cody Jerome's not the kind of guy runs from a fight. If I got to take on a bigger man, I'll give it a try, what the hell, it's no big thing to lose, right? Half the guys that mix got to lose. That's how it goes, so you quit when you find out you can't win and we all settle for that. But not with Bo. He's a guy wants to kill you. I saw him stomp a guy in Cranston once. I mean, with both feet, whomp! whomp! I'll never know how the poor bastard lived, but the fact he did sure wasn't Bo's fault. He tried his damnedest. I don't want any part of that bird, no sirree and thanks a lot."

"How come you gave his girl the rush?"

"Dumb. Plain, stupid, dumb. Didn't know she was his, for God's sake, never saw her with him. And she came on warm as an oven. I thought I was going to get laid, you know? I hadn't figured on getting laid out."

"Nobody warned you?"

"In Cranston? Hell no, I got no pals there. They'd watch me get stomped and die laughing."

"Why'd you start messing around when you'd brought your own girl?"

"Aw, come on! Don't tell me you never saw any fluff

that didn't look better than what you already had in your pocket."

"You saying you'd have ditched your date and her luggage?"

"Oh well, no, I wouldn't have left her without a ride." He glanced at Alma apologetically and grinned. "I didn't really think about any of it—all I knew was this babe was hot and I was ready. The stiff you-know-what's got no conscience, right?"

I couldn't claim mine did, but it wasn't something I was going to admit in front of the kid even though I was pretty sure she wasn't following what we said. It wasn't a thing I could assume because there was something all too knowing in those childish eyes.

"Any idea where Bo might stay in the Cities?" I asked. "He got any relatives there?"

"Relatives? That son of a bitch was probably hatched out of an egg buried in a sand bank, like a crocodile. All I know is, Sarah's nuts about dancing. If she gets her way, they'll probably be at some hall come Saturday. Or maybe they dance every day in the Cities. If I was him, I'd just keep her in a hotel for a week."

"Could he afford that?"

"Maybe. He always had something going on. Bo's the kind of guy borrows money and never pays it back. Been doing it since he was a kid. Protection money, you know?"

I asked Cody what he planned to do when he was back on his feet.

"I'm gonna talk old Brundage into hiring me in that bank. Been thinking about that steady the last couple days. The hell with screwing around—most business is a gamble, you know? Banking's sure."

"I seem to remember some going bust a couple years back."

"That won't happen again. Never. I've watched the way they operate and kept a steady eye on old Brundage. Guys like him don't go bust. That's for me. Use the old noodle, diddle the crowd. Hell, it's a license to steal. Nobody messes with them. Not the cops or the feds or anybody but some dumb-asses that try to rob the place and get themselves run down and shot sooner and later. Believe me, pal, money's the thing. People go to church to pray, but they worship at the bank."

I wished I could get him to lecture Ma on that subject but suspected even Cody Jerome couldn't steamroller her. Still it was a duel I'd like to watch.

I asked him if he'd ever planned to marry Winnie. His face went blank and he said, "Huh?" although I was certain he'd heard me. I repeated the question.

"Well, sure," he said, almost before I'd finished asking. "It was just one of those things we never got around to, you know?"

"You talk about it?"

"Oh yeah. Just never got around to setting a date."

"Did she ever tell you that her husband's father had disowned him?"

He waved his good arm. "Winnie never talked about his old man. I suppose he was pretty much a bastard—the old man, I mean."

"How'd you like Ellsworth?"

"I liked him. He was nuts, but okay. Never gave us any trouble. Most guys in his shoes, they'd have been snotty as hell and all that stuff. Old Ellsworth, he'd grin at me and say, 'How're you doing?' and I'd say 'Everybody I could,' and he'd nod and keep on drinking."

I thanked him for talking with me, and he said, hey, it'd been his pleasure, come around any time, and take good care of the little princess.

Back outside I picked her up and carried her on my shoulders. She hung on to my ears at first, but before we'd gone a block she was resting one hand on my head. People we met smiled at me and waved at her and she waved back.

It was fun.

15

I left Alma at the Leighs' well before supper and went back to City Hall, where Al was listening to a citizen beef about some kid who'd motorcycled through town at sixty per. Al granted it was a crime but pointed out that by the time he could get his Model T started the guy'd already be in Aquatown and maybe a little hard to find.

The citizen left, unmollified, and Al stared at me glumly when I sat down.

"What've you found out about Bo?" I asked.

"Diddly-squat."

"You know anybody'd have a picture of him?"

"No. Why?"

I said I was thinking about a trip to Minneapolis and it might help if I knew what the guy I was looking for looked like. He told me he didn't figure such a trip would be either educational or morally uplifting.

"You ever been there?" he asked.

"Yup."

"Didn't do you any good, did it?"

"Yeah. It solved a murder."

He snorted. "I suppose that time you were looking for a guy you couldn't recognize and didn't have an address for?"

"I had an address. It didn't make any difference if I could recognize him because he got knocked off before I reached him."

"That sounds about like Minneapolis these days. Gettin' as bad as Chicago."

"What kind of a guy's Odie Frye?"

"Odie? He's okay, except if talking people to death was a crime he'd be serving life. Why?"

"He told me Ellsworth was feeling smug his last night."

"Uh-huh. Just keep in mind that anybody with as much to talk about as Odie has just naturally got to make up a lot of what he thinks he knows."

"You think he's a windbag?"

"Not always. What else'd he tell you?"

"He said Ellsworth told him it was better to work for an open crook than a closed one. He's not sure whether that meant he liked working for Brundage or Winnie's old man most. All that's clear is he doesn't believe Ellsworth preferred the judge."

Al scowled and hitched around in his chair. "That's the kind of bullshit you get from Odie. It's typical of Ellsworth, too. He's the kind of guy'd diddle you around to agreeing with him and then grin and say, 'You said it, I didn't.' Made me madder than hell."

I considered asking if it made him mad enough to nudge Ellsworth into a moving train but decided it wouldn't amuse him much.

"Ever hear any stories about people having problems with the judge back when he was a lawyer?" I asked.

He looked at me sharply. "What're you getting at?"

"I've heard about how now and again the lawyer gets more out of a legacy or a lawsuit than the heir or the client."

He crossed his thick legs and frowned. "You got something special in mind?"

"How about Winnie? Or her ma?"

"You got things mixed up. The judge's brother, Sam, handled them."

"They were partners then, weren't they?"

He admitted that was so and thought for a while.

"I don't think there was ever that much money involved. Winnie's old man sure didn't make any of his loot here. 'Course he could've brought some along—it took a pretty good layout of cash to buy their house, even on time."

"He get a loan from Brundage?"

"That was before Brundage's time. The loan would've been with Rutledge's bank. It went bust."

"Rutledge still around?"

"Yeah, but he'd be hard to talk to. They buried him after he killed himself. Anyway, Winnie's ma more than likely fiddled away any money she was left. She was a ding-dong, that one."

Men in our territory never figured women had any money sense. I accepted that for years before it dawned on me that in my own family it was the old man who bought phony gold stocks and Ma who saved dimes and socked them in the bank. And it was the men who bought fancy cars that wore out or got wrecked while the women tried to furnish homes, and the only money they wasted was when they bought clothes and costume jewelry trying to look good to catch a man or keep him. I figured out that the main thing keeping women down was they mostly had this notion they needed a man.

I went back to Leighs' for supper and found Evangeline with Annabelle and the doc in the living room. Alma came downstairs as soon as she heard me and got in my lap.

Evangeline asked what I'd learned in Aquatown. I said that Cody'd been converted. Both women raised their eyebrows.

"To what?" asked Doc.

"Banking."

They looked blank at that, and I explained how Cody had decided to change his way of life and concentrate on money instead of specializing in girls and good times.

"Some conversion," said Annabelle.

"Cody said I might find Bo and his wife in one of the dance halls if I went to the Cities."

Evangeline's head raised at that, and Annabelle scowled at her, then at me. "Why'd you mention that?" she demanded.

"I thought maybe Evangeline'd offer me a ride to the Cities, like she did to Cranston. My car's still not fixed."

Annabelle stood up, scraping her chair back. "That's the most ridiculous proposal I ever heard of. It was foolish driving to Cranston; it'd be insane going all the way to Minneapolis."

"I suppose it'd cause talk," I admitted.

"You think I'm scared to?" asked Evangeline.

"Oh no, but you'd probably better talk it over with the judge."

"I don't have to talk it over with anybody. If I want to go, I'll do it. I'm not a child."

"You talk like one," said her sister.

"Well," I said as they glared at each other, "there's no hurry to decide. I won't go until Saturday. That's when they have dances, right?"

Annabelle glared at her silent husband, then turned it on me. I looked at him. His sad face looked longer and

more tired than usual and I had the sudden feeling the
healer was sick.

"Aren't you going to say anything?" Annabelle
demanded of her husband.

"Well . . ." he began.

Annabelle hiked for the stairs. Doc, looking fussed,
got up and followed her. Evangeline and I sat in silence
for a few seconds before she got up and walked to the
foot of the stairs, where she stood a few moments.

"The trouble with Annabelle," she said when she
returned, "is she never hollers. It'd make things easier
for her if she could, I think."

I guessed it'd make her easier to hear, too, and started
to roll a cigarette under Alma's watchful stare, thought
better of it, and shoved the tobacco bag into my shirt
pocket.

"You really raise the devil everywhere you go, don't
you," said Evangeline.

"I usually get lots of help."

"Yes," she sighed, "I sure didn't improve things."
After a second she narrowed her eyes at me. "Is your car
really not fixed?"

"Not as I know of."

"You haven't even checked, have you? You want to go
in a bigger, better car. One not so easy to push off the
road."

"It's a good point, but I never thought of it. I just
wanted company. It's a long drive."

"Oh sure. What'd you do for company when you were
a hobo?"

"There were always other hobos. That's the real
reason I gave up the business. How about we go out on
the back stoop where I can roll a smoke?"

Evangeline looked at Alma and decided she'd be a safe chaperone. "Okay."

But we had just got comfortable with Alma between us and my cigarette lit when the doc showed up at the screen and told Evangeline her sister wanted to see her up in the bedroom. Evangeline sighed again and went.

Doc Leigh came out and stood over us. "You want a beer?"

I nodded.

He went back in the kitchen and returned with two opened bottles, handed me one, and sat down. Alma raised her hands and I told her to take a sniff. She did, made a face, and settled back.

Two or three times Doc seemed about to speak, but nothing came out so I asked what was he supposed to tell me.

He looked sheepish, sat up straighter, and braced his palms on the stoop. "You have to remember," he began, "that Annabelle's always been a second mother to Evangeline. She's felt that her little sister looked up to her, respected her opinions, and took her advice. That's been very important to Annabelle."

"Sounds like she needs a kid of her own."

Instead of getting sore he nodded wearily. "I've certainly thought of that. I've even felt that Alma's tragedy might be a kind of blessing for us, that she'd be like a gift. But so far there's not been the acceptance you might expect. It's like you've come in the way. That's pretty bad, you know? But what's worse, you seem to be taking Evangeline away, too. Annabelle sees this business of going to Minneapolis as a total disaster, not only to her little sister's reputation and future, but to their relationship. You really shouldn't be doing this."

He looked at me directly and I tried a swig of the beer. It wasn't cold and tasted bitter.

"You think the little sister ought to stick around this town all her life, taking care of her old uncle till he croaks?"

"I think that's unlikely."

"It's a lot more likely than the notion she'll be shunned into a convent if she drives me to the Cities."

"Well," he said after a moment, "she's got a cousin she could stay with in Minneapolis."

Alma was sleepy and I thought of taking her up to bed but postponed it. I didn't want the women thinking I was trying to listen in on them. I tried the beer again and looked at Doc.

"A guy who claims he knew Ellsworth says he sort of hinted the judge was a crook. Any idea why?"

Doc shook his head and put his beer down. "No. He's a politician—I guess that automatically makes a man suspect to some types. The judge cultivates friendships and knows how to compromise. Those practices would be anathema to a man like Ellsworth, but I doubt that he'd actually say it made him a *crook*."

"How about his brother Sam, your father-in-law?"

"He had a very sound reputation. I can't claim to have known him intimately—he was never a doting father— just a good lawyer and pretty serious. Less colorful than the judge. They were close and Sam helped get Cal elected to the bench."

"You mean he spent money on it?"

"You don't buy judgeships in Toqueville."

I said pardon me without much sarcasm and he frowned a little before asking if I wanted another beer. I shook my head.

Evangeline opened the door and stood over us. "You going to keep that child up all night?" she demanded.

It wasn't a question meant for an answer. I got up carefully and carried Alma to her bed. She didn't even mutter when I left the room.

Doc and Evangeline had moved to the living room when I came down. She asked me what time I wanted to start for the Cities on Saturday.

"We need about eight or ten hours. Say we start at seven?"

"We'll bring Alma along. I can leave her at my cousin's."

"That okay with Annabelle?"

"What difference does that make?"

"I like to keep peace in the family."

"Oh sure, you're real good at that. I haven't changed my mind about you, you know. I still think you sold Uncle Cal out. I'm just going on this trip to keep an eye on you. If you don't like that notion, say so right now."

"You can keep anything on me but a leash," I told her.

She looked at Doc. "You think he's honest, don't you?"

He looked back at her, frowning. "Basically, yes."

"Basically?" She glared at me. "Usually he's good at judging people but in your case I'm not convinced. I wish I were." I let that hang, and she shook her head in exasperation. "You never defend yourself, do you? Can't you say something?"

"I got nothing to defend. At least not in this case, so far."

That didn't warm her up any and after fuming around without saying much she told us good night and left.

The doc and I got up and stood a moment considering the problem of womankind. Finally, he shook his head and said, "You're going to have quite a trip."

He was right.

16

I called Minneapolis in the morning, trying to locate the detective who'd invited me never to return the last time I visited his town. He wasn't easy to find because I'd never caught his name. The guy who answered the telephone had little imagination but my description finally brought results.

His name was Logan.

He laughed when he remembered me and said sure, he wasn't about to forget the guy who creamed a killer with a toilet tank cover. "What're you using for a weapon these days?"

I said a fast retreat and he laughed again. He told me the guy I'd clobbered was still in prison and likely to stay, since he'd killed another con the first month he was in. "So," he said, "you got a new playmate?"

I told him about Bo. He said the guy sounded like pretty small potatoes for a giant-killer like me. He was determined to be very funny. When he'd had his laughs I asked if he could check on whether anybody from Toqueville or Cranston had put in an inquiry about Bo.

He thought that over for a couple seconds. "You figure the local cops aren't too eager to run him down?"

"I'd just like to make sure."

"Uh-huh. You want to be careful asking questions like that about a cop. Especially to another cop. Us profes-

133

sionals got to cover each other's ass, you know. Just like doctors."

I didn't comment and he quit trying to be funny.

"Okay. Call back after lunch. I'll nose around."

I went to the café for breakfast and before my order was filled Percy popped out of the kitchen and said the judge wanted me to call. Right away. I said I'd take care of it after I ate. Percy shook his head and went back in the kitchen.

Right after my pancakes arrived, officer Al Jacobsen showed up. He greeted the waitress and six or seven customers before he made a show of noticing me and strolled over to take the stool on my right. He ordered coffee and stared at me in the mirror while he waited for it to be poured. I kept eating.

"You don't take advice too good, do you?" he said.

"A man doesn't have to take advice."

He gave up the mirror and turned to give me the hard eye. "I'm beginning to think you're not too smart, Wilcox."

"Never made any claims in that line."

"You're gonna be crossing state lines, you know. There's a law about that."

"Only when it's for carnal purposes. You figure I'm going to sell the lady? Or she's gonna sell herself?"

"She don't know her own mind. She's young and headstrong—"

"And over twenty-one."

"That don't make any damned difference."

"It does to her. And I didn't hypnotize her or even fast-talk her into it. There were witnesses. There's nothing sneaky about the whole business, so what's your problem?"

He leaned close and talked low. "You listen. I talked to you before, man to man, because I figured you were man enough to understand I was talking sense. Now it looks like you're just total contrary, bound to make all the trouble you can just to get into that girl's pants. There's no other reason for you to go off to the Cities with her, and you sure as hell won't make it better by taking along that kid. For God's sake, if anything, that makes it worse."

"Why?"

"Well, goddamnit, it ain't natural. . . ."

"Is it illegal?"

He settled back and managed to calm down enough to try his coffee. After a couple swallows he put the cup down very carefully, as if it might shatter from his anger.

"Mr. Wilcox, I can damned sure find it a crime if that's how you want it. You got a record. Like it or lump it, that makes you different from other men. Maybe it ain't fair, but you're a big boy now and you know fair's not worth *shit*. Right?"

I admitted it.

"All right. So don't pull any of that stockade-lawyer shit on me. You and me, we been around. We talk to each other, we don't have to go through a lot of bullshit, right?"

"Right. Tell you what. You talk to Brundage. If he says I lay off this case, okay, I'll lay off. If he says go, I go all the way."

He stared at me for a few seconds, pulled back, looked around, caught the waitress's eye, which was easy since every soul in the place was watching us like they expected a gunfight, and waved his coffee cup.

I finished my pancakes, drank some coffee, and we

both lit up smokes. A few customers left. The ones remaining went back to talking with each other while keeping one eye our way. There was a hush in the place, like a funeral parlor at showtime.

When I got up Al rose too, and we went out to the street together. The bright sun warmed us and the wind whipped dust off the graveled street, making us squint as we walked toward City Hall.

"I'm supposed to call the judge," I told him. "Can I use your phone?"

He nodded glumly.

I made the call while he went back to check on the drunk in the lone cell. Evangeline answered on the first ring.

"I heard the judge wants me," I said.

She took a deep breath. "Just try not to make him any madder than he already is, okay?"

I heard him breathing a time or two before he spoke and then he just said, "Carl?"

"Yup."

"Carl, I want you to explain to me, if you will, exactly what you expect to accomplish with this trip you're planning with my niece and little Alma."

"I'm going to look up Bo and hear what he's got to say about the fracas last Saturday night."

"To what end? You already told me such a trip would be useless and I agreed."

"It would be, as far as you're concerned."

"I don't understand your reasoning. It seemed before that you were satisfied he caused the accident but didn't expect to prove it. Surely you don't suddenly expect him to make a confession when you confront him?"

"I plan to crowd him a little."

"Don't be ridiculous. You've hired out to Brundage and intend to do anything that'll embarrass or upset me because that's what'd please Brundage and earn your pay. That's all this comes down to."

"No it isn't. What interests everybody is what happened to Ellsworth. He worked for you and Brundage, and nobody in town's been able to tell me why either one of you guys'd hire and put up with a drunk."

"What in the pluperfect hell has Ellsworth got to do with Bo Grummen and this trip you're taking with Evangeline?"

"Maybe nothing. But there's something fishy about that accident and I want to talk to Bo about it."

"So why take my niece along?"

"I'm not taking her, Judge. She offered to drive."

"That's nonsense. You've tricked her into doing it to spite me and defy Al Jacobsen. That's the truth and you know it."

He hung up on me, and when I looked up Al was leaning against the doorjamb. We watched each other a moment before he came in, shook his head, and sat down. "I wish I thought you was just bullheaded and dumb," he said.

"Yeah? What do you think I am?"

"Deep, stubborn, and maybe mean. I wish I'd never seen you."

"My old man has a saying about wishes. He says wish in one hand and crap in the other and see which gets full first."

That didn't double him up any—he just kept staring glumly.

I asked if he'd really called Minneapolis to ask the cops about Bo.

"What makes you think I haven't?"

"You haven't said anything that'd make me think you had."

"You figure I got a reason not to?"

"Maybe you're shy and don't want to talk to big-city cops. Or maybe you don't want to find him. Maybe somebody in town doesn't want the man found at all."

"You're just fulla maybes, aren't you? How about maybe you tell me what the the hell you're getting at besides calling me a liar. What the hell's Bo got to do with anything Mr. Brundage hired you to do?"

"I won't know till I talk to him. I might not know then."

"You're damned right you won't know then. Bo's no more going to talk with you than turn Christian. He'll more likely kill you."

"Well, I guess that wouldn't break your heart."

"It sure as hell wouldn't. Come on, gimme one reason why he'd tell you anything but go to hell."

"He might not want to take the rap for murder all by himself."

He stared at me, shook his head, and said I was crazy.

I about half figured he was right. But I wanted to see and hear the man, find out how he'd react to me head-on. I didn't expect a confession or alibi—just a better idea of what I was up against. Of all the people I'd met or heard about since finding the Dodge smashed into that clay bank, only Bo seemed genuinely dangerous. The first-hand life-and-death man.

The rest of the day went slow. I went to see Alma and Annabelle wouldn't let me in the door. She sent Alma out and told me to take her over to the judge's yard. I didn't argue with her. While I was pushing my small friend on the swing I saw Arnie Bridstand approach the judge's house and figured he was coming around for a last shot at making Evangeline see the light. A little later I glimpsed him heading back toward the hotel. He looked whipped.

When Evangeline came out and sat on the back stoop, I left Alma playing in the sandpile and went over to visit with her.

"I feel like a poop," she told me.

"Why's that?"

"Well, it isn't enough all my family's mad at me, half the town is, too. It'd be flattering if it weren't so ridiculous. They all act like I held the honor of Toqueville in my lily-white hands."

"That's the disadvantage of an unblemished past."

She shook her head and looked at me. "You never went through that, huh?"

"Not that I can remember. The first thing I ever heard was that I was no good."

"Who told you that?"

"My old man."

"And you spent the rest of your life trying to live up to that, right?"

"It was never a chore."

She stared at the grass beside her feet. "I'm glad my mother isn't around. This whole business would have killed her."

"If she was around, this whole business probably wouldn't have happened."

"I think maybe so. Things have just come to where I've got to do what *I* want to. I will not live my life just to please everybody else. I want out of this town. I'm sick of it and the gossip and maliciousness. When we get to Minneapolis I'm going to see if I can get a job. Or maybe I'll go to school. I could, you know. I did real well in classes, and I could stay with my cousin—she doesn't live far from the university."

"Doesn't that cost?"

"I could sell my car and work part-time."

"You've got the title?"

"Uh-huh. Uncle Cal gave it to me when I came to stay. It was a present. There was no obligation with it."

She could see I wasn't buying that and decided to change the subject.

"Look, you won't try to pull anything on this trip, will you? I mean, I'm not running off with you for an affair or anything like that. You understand, don't you?"

"It'll be whatever way you want it."

"That's the way I want it. You've got to understand and accept that. I'm not loose, you know."

I said I never figured she was.

"Uncle Cal says this trip is a wild-goose chase, that you won't find Bo and even if you do he won't tell you anything and if you're right about him doing something awful, he'll probably kill you. He's a lot bigger than you and he's got those big ape friends."

I said it certainly did sound discouraging.

"But you're stubborn, just like me, so you'll go anyway."

"That's right."

She grinned, then apparently regretted it and said, "I still don't trust you. You're very devious under that good-old-hobo exterior. You've got plans and that's okay, but forget about getting anywhere with me the minute we're out of town or any other time. I just wish I knew what you've got in mind to do about Bo."

"Planning's not my specialty," I told her. "I just figure things'll come to me if I let them happen. That doesn't always work, but I got to be where it can happen or it won't. You see?"

She looked across the yard at Alma, who was pushing sand into a small mountain. "Well," she said, "I hope you'll be careful. Us girls need you."

17

After lunch at Percy's I called the Minneapolis detective, Logan.

"Nobody here's heard from your man about this guy Bo Grummen," he told me. "We've checked hotels, but if he's around he's staying with friends or using an alias."

I thanked him and he asked was I planning to visit the Cities. I admitted I'd been thinking about it.

"Drop around. I'll buy you a cup of coffee."

"Last time I was around you told me not to come back."

"Back then I didn't know how much your stumbling around managed to help us out. We owe you."

I thanked him and went back to the Leighs'. Nobody answered my knock, so I looked in the judge's backyard and found Annabelle on the stoop with a cup of coffee watching Alma in the sandbox. Annabelle had given her some doll dishes and a table and Alma had them all set up on the leveled sand and was having a coffee party for Raggedy Ann, who took it all in with dollish indifference.

"Evangeline," Annabelle told me, "is really, right down deep, afraid of men. That's why she's attracted to you."

I said I didn't get that.

"It's perfectly simple. You're all male. You've traveled a lot, fought men, had lots of women, mixed with murderers. You're everything she fears and she hates being afraid, won't give in to it, and makes her life miserable fighting it all. That's why she went with Cody Jerome and let him teach her to drive. She didn't like *him*, she was afraid of him, so of course she went out with him and when he tried to do what she was afraid of, she fought him off. She'll do the same to you."

"She won't have to fight me off."

"She will, in her own way. You'll see."

"Okay. She'll drive me there, go to her cousin's, and when I've done what I'm going to do she can pick me up and we'll drive home again."

She shook her head. "She plans on being with you. She says you don't know Bo and she does and she'll identify him for you. If she insists on staying with you, how'll you stop her? You going to knock her down?"

I admitted that was unlikely.

"You think you can stay in control. The tough guy. Well, you can't. Evangeline's a very determined and stubborn girl and everybody in the family knows it and you'll find out."

That took some color off the blossom, which was, of course, exactly what Annabelle aimed for. I grinned at her and she glowered at me. Then Alma got up, abandoned her party, and came over to us. Annabelle finished her cup, got up, went to pick up the party in the sandbox, and headed back to her house after telling me to take Alma for a walk.

We strolled down to the park and watched kids playing ball for a while before Duke Peterson and Arnie Bridstand came around and stood in front of us, blocking my view of the game. I didn't pretend that was important. Duke looked sour, Arnie was more like anxious.

"You always got a woman or a kid with you, haven't you?" said Duke.

"I've led a lonely life. I'm trying to make up for it in your friendly town."

"What you're doing," he said, "is hiding behind kids and women. You know if you tried to take Evie in your own car to the Cities, you'd never make it out of town."

"You'd bust up the Tin Lizzie again, huh?"

"Damn right."

"I figured you for it."

"You going to tell the cop?"

"If I told anybody it'd be the guy who paid for the repair. I'm glad you're too much a man of honor to mess up a lady's car."

"If it weren't for Arnie here, I'd have messed *you* up."

"You already tried that once, without much luck."

"You caught me by surprise. That won't happen again."

"You try again, son, and you won't walk away."

He started to flare but Arnie put one hand on his arm and he settled back on his heels.

"You want somebody to identify Bo," said Arnie, "I'll come along with you."

I sighed. "Arnie, quit dreaming. Evangeline wants to drive me to the Cities. You want her to stay home, talk to her. Who the hell you think I'm going to try and please? You? The judge? Or the lady? Why the hell should I get her mad at me?"

"To keep out of trouble," said Duke.

"It'd be for her own good," said Arnie. "She'd appreciate it in the long run."

"I'm not a distance runner. Now move over and let us watch the game."

Arnie had to step in front of Duke to stop him, and for a few seconds I thought they were going to mix it but pretty quick they moved off.

I looked down at Alma, who stared at me with a quivering chin and finally said, "Home."

"You watched guys mad at each other before, didn't you?" I said.

She nodded.

"Don't worry. Nothing's going to happen."

She wasn't convinced. I picked her up and jounced her a little as I walked along and told her we'd sing "Row, Row, Row Your Boat" in the car tomorrow. She still looked scared. I assured her it would be light out and no one would chase us.

When I took Alma home, Annabelle told me to come around later for supper.

It was mostly a silent meal except when Annabelle was trying to coax Alma into eating. We had a hot dish made with hamburger and it didn't appeal to me any more than it did to her but I still ate my share. I kept wondering if the choice of food came from Annabelle's being sore at me.

Up on the bed later, I asked Alma if she remembered Cody Jerome and Bo arguing. She put her hands over her ears.

I hugged her and told the story of how I once painted the town of Corden red by climbing the water tower and splashing paint all over the light. I didn't tell her I was drunk, of course. She liked my description of everybody looking up with faces reflecting red. That wasn't enough to make her go to sleep, so I told her about the time Pa and Ma were living in Missouri and Pa brought home a pail full of blackberries and hid them on top of the kitchen shelves when Ma was outside, and when she came in right away spotted the pail up where it didn't belong. She was so crazy about blackberries she cried when he finally took them down for her to see.

Downstairs I found Al Jacobsen in the kitchen with Doc and Annabelle. I figured at first he was planning to throw me in jail, but he only nodded when I sat down and accepted coffee. The conversation didn't go anywhere and I finally said I was going back to the hotel. Al said he'd walk with me.

As soon as we got out in the quiet night I spotted the car down the street a ways. It was too dark to see who was inside but I felt sure it was Duke's flivver.

"What's this?" I asked Al. "You giving me a police escort or are you going to back up the local boys?"

"I'm gonna walk you over to the hotel. Don't try to make anything of it."

I said I didn't plan to, but I sure thought about what I'd do if the car pulled alongside and Al moved in back of me. Not a lot of bright ideas came along.

The car started up and followed us. Al didn't look back.

"You've heard some talk?" I suggested.

"Yeah."

"So what do you care?"

"Not a whole hell of a lot. Like I said, I don't want you busting up the local citizenry."

"I don't suppose you've been talking with Brundage?"

He gave me a dirty look. "I don't work for Brundage."

"How about the judge?"

"You trying to make me mad?"

"No. Just think some. You didn't call Minneapolis, did you?"

"No I didn't. I don't work for you, either. And don't tell me I don't work at all. I do my own job my own way and nobody's complained that counts."

"Well, in that case I'd say you've performed a miracle and I'd genuflect but it might make my knees pop."

We reached the hotel and I stopped to face him. He'd made up his mind he wasn't going to get mad no matter what, so I gave up ragging him.

"You know how Winnie's old man made his wad?" I asked.

"I'd guess he sold snake oil or the like to folks down South and some West. One of them medicines that's mostly alcohol."

"But he didn't sell any here?"

"Never. Just retired, took sick, and died. I'd guess he was sick when they came."

"And he built a big house. What happened to it?"

"Wife sold it pretty quick after he died. Took a loss, I understand. Bud Cranston, son of Cranston's founder, bought it." He added some ancient history I didn't care about and eventually I got him back to Winnie's ma and the house.

"You know the judge's brother handled the sale?"

"Seems more like it was the judge. Why?"

"Curious. Anybody know if Ellsworth's family ever tried to get to him while he was here?"

"Not that I know of. You trying to find out if little

Alma's got a bundle coming somewhere? That why you're cozying up to her?''

"You got it, Al. I always wanted to marry money. 'Course she's a little young, but she'll get over that.''

He snorted. "Don't make any big plans. The talk about money in that family is more'n likely hot air. The claims about Ellsworth being some kind of smart freak is probably more of the same. Don't forget, old Amos was a snake-oil salesman and he was the guy that started all the stories about Ellsworth.''

I figured he'd leave me at the hotel door but he walked in behind me. Arnie wasn't in sight. The old man was sitting in a rocker near the registration desk and looked up from his *Liberty* magazine, blinked, and set it aside.

Al greeted him, he responded with a nod, got up, and limped over to look out in the street.

"Arnie's in Duke's car, about a block east,'' Al told him.

The old man returned to his chair without comment.

There was some more talk between Al and me without any education for either of us, and I went up to my room. I didn't ask if Al planned to stand guard all night in the lobby.

I was stretched out on the bed, still dressed, when there was a knock on the door. I got up, walked close, and stood to one side. "Yeah?''

"Wilcox, I want to talk to you,'' said Brundage.

I opened the door, he came in, looked around suspiciously, gave the straight-backed chair a glance, sat down, and leaned forward with his hands braced on his knees.

"It seems to me,'' he said, "that we had a clear

understanding that I was to know and approve any trips you made."

"I haven't made any."

"You're making one tomorrow. With the judge's niece and Alma. You deny that?"

"Nope."

"What's the point? And why with the girl and child?"

"To see Bo. Talk to him. And Evangeline's driving me for free and Alma's coming along because Annabelle wants it that way."

"Why didn't you discuss this with me?"

"It's not going to cost you, so why worry?"

He sat straight, folded his arms, and scowled. "You're forgetting something. I hired you. People in town know that. They assume I condone your activities. When you turn the job I hired you for into a flaming affair, I'm going to get burned. You can act like an idiot and that girl can play loose and it won't matter to either of you, but I'm a banker and I have to answer to the community and keep my reputation."

"You didn't worry about that when you hired Ellsworth."

"That was different."

"Okay. You want to fire me?"

"I want to know what the devil is going on."

"You already know. I'm going to find Bo. If I do, I'll tell you what happened when I get back."

"*If* you get back."

"There's always that."

He got up, moved to the door, and scowled back at me. "I wish I could trust you. I don't. You lack good judgment and you're tricky."

"I'd guess you'd be good at spotting that."

"You're making a mortal enemy of the judge, you know."

"So've you and you've survived."

"The situation for me is quite different."

"Yeah, everything's different for everybody. I'll drop around when I get back."

18

We were a couple miles out of Toqueville when I sighted the trailing car. It wasn't Duke's jalopy, and when I mentioned the car to Evangeline she squinted in the mirror and asked if I could read the license plate. I could.

"That's a Cranston number—or at least their county."

"So it's Tucker, Fisher, and McCall, Bo's gang."

She drove in silence for a few moments and then asked if I thought we should circle back home.

"It's your car."

"I don't think theirs'll go any faster than mine."

"Also it's not night and we're not on a back road."

"But there's not much traffic."

"Well, work it out to suit yourself."

She glanced at Alma, who sat between us, leaning against my side. "She shouldn't go through another experience like the last."

We drove in silence as I watched the following car. It stayed about a hundred yards behind us. Evangeline held the speedometer needle at a steady fifty.

We stopped at a small café in a little town on the border of Minnesota for a late breakfast. As we left our car the big Buick rolled on by. I could see the three guys in front with Mac at the wheel. Mac was grinning but didn't look our way. None of them did.

Our stocky blond waitress gave Alma lots of attention and brought us pancakes, bacon, coffee, and milk. We were just starting to eat when the three guys came in and sat in a row at the counter. They ordered coffee and stared at us in the mirror. I was glad Alma had her back to them.

Mac kept grinning. His two partners just tried to look tough. They were pretty good at it. I thought about who might have given them the word about our trip but it was hopeless, since everybody in Toqueville knew our plans.

"Are those the fellows you made friends with on our last trip?" Evangeline asked me.

I nodded.

"You couldn't have found any bigger, could you?"

I told her I couldn't pick Bo's friends for him.

"Maybe," she said, "when we leave here I'd just better take off and see if we can outrun them."

Alma looked at her, then at me.

"Let's not panic the troops," I said.

She looked a little flustered and sipped her coffee very casually. "Maybe," she said after a moment, "I should make a call to Al."

"That wouldn't get us anywhere. The simplest thing is to drive back."

Alma quit eating. Evangeline ate carefully and, after a few bites, urged Alma to finish her breakfast. The little girl picked at the pancakes but couldn't quite get into it. After a while she drank a little milk at my urging.

I looked around for the toilet and saw it was at the end of the counter in back. No help. There was probably a door from the kitchen to the alley, but if I headed that way the gang was sure to follow.

"What I need," I told Evangeline, "is a crack at their car."

"You want me to distract them?"

"I don't think anything short of a striptease on the counter would swing it. You willing to try?"

She shook her head impatiently and, after a moment, leaned toward me with new anxiety. "What if they've done something to *my* car?"

"Uh-uh. I can see it through the window. They didn't go near it."

She sat back firmly. "All right. Let them follow. I can outrun them."

Mac finished his coffee, stood, hitched up his pants, and leaned over to whisper in Fisher's ear. Fisher nodded. Mac grinned our way and strolled to the cash register. His partners followed, paid, and trooped out. For a moment they stood on the sidewalk, gazing at Evangeline's Oldsmobile. Pretty soon they had a good laugh and walked west.

We paid our bill and went outside. The Buick was parked a quarter of a block away, idling quietly.

We walked to the Olds and got in. The motor started easily and Evangeline leaned back and turned to me.

"Maybe we could find someone here to leave Alma with."

"No!" cried Alma, and she struggled to her feet and grabbed me.

"It'd only be for a day, honey," said Evangeline.

"No!" screamed Alma, clutching me.

I gathered her in and told her not to worry, I wouldn't leave her anywhere.

Evangeline muttered angrily about only thinking of the

child's own good, put the car in reverse, jerked us back, slammed the transmission into low, and peeled off, heading east. The Buick followed a mite more sedately.

As soon as we hit the highway I noticed the telephone poles were getting closer and closer together along the roadside. I figured as soon as they looked like a picket fence I was going to ask the lady to ease off.

The yellow road ran its thin gold line across the prairie between brown fields of wheat and spindly corn, occasional pale farmhouse, and faded red barns. Ahead, the road narrowed to a needle point on the horizon under a pale blue sky. Now and again I'd spot a few bony cows in a baked pasture and the ones close to the fence would lift their wide heads and stare vacantly as we whipped by.

We crested a hill and streaked down into a wide, shallow valley that stretched forever, all laid out in squares of county roads, with less than a dozen lonely farmhouses scattered in isolation, lifeless as an oil-painted landscape.

I looked back. "They're gaining," I warned Evangeline.

She leaned forward and the Olds surged ahead. Very gradually the gap between us and the trailing Buick opened up again.

"They're trying to panic you," I said.

"They're good at it."

Alma pressed hard against me with her face flat against my side.

We raced across the valley floor, passed a truck so fast I doubt the driver saw us, crested the next hill, and sighted a small town straddling the graveled highway.

Evangeline's eyes narrowed, trying to take in the place

at a glance, then whisked us through without easing off the gas pedal. The Buick hung on. I looked beyond it and couldn't see a soul in the dwindling town.

"You hoping to pick up a cop?" I asked.

"You got a better idea?"

I didn't.

"Got a map?" I asked. She nodded toward the glove compartment. I dug it out and spread it on my lap after gently nudging Alma over.

"What're you looking for?" asked Evangeline.

"The next decent-sized town. We're gonna need gas."

"I've still got half a tank."

"That won't get us to the Cities."

She glanced in the mirror and leaned harder on the gas.

"If we find a town big enough to be safe for that, we'll find a cop that'll help."

That made sense, but I didn't like it. I don't feel comfortable with strange cops and, even worse, I don't want them doing me favors. Except for Joey, once they know anything about me they aren't so inclined.

She said she didn't care what I thought, the next town we hit with anybody alive in sight, she was going to park in front of City Hall and get help.

I didn't argue.

But when we reached the next big town the Buick was nowhere in sight. They'd fallen back when we'd reached the outskirts.

We drove down Main Street and saw live people on the sidewalk and a couple of cars moving. Evangeline found City Hall, pulled up in front, and turned off the engine.

"Before we go in," I said, "what's our story?"

"We're being followed by three men in a car who're threatening us."

"Fine. Only we can't point any three guys out. And if we could, what'd we say to explain why these guys are following us?"

"What's the difference *why?*"

"Because that's the kind of stuff cops want to know all about. A cop is going to ask what makes you think these guys are chasing us and if you don't make the story good he's going to get suspicious as hell and he's going to ask more questions and the more he asks the less he's going to believe."

"The trouble with you," she said, "is you don't trust police."

"I know how they think and how they work, and if you think about it just a little bit you'll know I'm right. And if you get this cop to call Toqueville and he talks with Al or your uncle, you think either one of those guys'll say anything that will do anything but make this cop keep us around?"

"You'd rather risk our lives than be embarrassed or kept waiting?"

We glared at each other and tried to ignore Alma, who for the moment seemed to want it that way.

"Okay, lady," I said. "It's your car and your neck. Do what you want."

"You think I'm chicken."

"No. You're being smart."

"You're getting sarcastic again. You think I'm chicken."

I denied it again, but she started the engine, backed into the street, and started off. She found a gas station on the edge of town, told the man to fill the tank, and went off to the ladies' room towing Alma along.

"You happen to notice a black Buick go by here a few minutes back?" I asked the attendant. He was a blond kid with a pimple like a sprouting horn on his forehead.

"Oh yah. Stopped for gas. Friends of yours?"

"Sort of. They head east?"

"Yah."

When Evangeline returned with Alma I spread the map on the hood and showed her the setup. "We're in Montevideo. Been following two-twelve. So what we do, we take this straight road, route seven, and go by way of Clara City and Cosmos."

"What if they've figured out we might do that and they're waiting there?"

"We'll think of something else."

She shook her head and looked east. "Why're they following us at all?"

"Trying to scare us off. Or maybe just having fun on a day off. If they don't scare us off or panic us into an accident, they'll go on to Minneapolis, look up Bo, and be around to help him out."

"So you'll be dealing with four toughs instead of one?"

"Yeah, well, I might be able to recruit a little help."

"Like who?"

"A Minneapolis cop or two."

"I thought you didn't trust cops?"

"I told you, I know a little about how they think and work. I know this Minneapolis guy and his partner. In a way, I helped them out once. I think they'd get a kick out of this deal."

She thought it over as I folded up the map and looked down at Alma. "Okay, honey, shall we keep going?"

Alma looked at me. I nodded. She looked back at Evangeline and nodded.

"Good Lord," said Evangeline, "you're turning her into a ventriloquist's dummy."

We found the alternate highway and set off. The Buick didn't show up.

19

The cousin lived in the lower level of a Minneapolis duplex off Lake Street. I parked in back by a garage set parallel with the alley, and we climbed four steps to the back entry hall. The inside door opened before Evangeline could knock, and a small woman with hair like a red halo darted out and grabbed her in a vigorous hug. After a second she let go and crouched to greet Alma, who looked back into her pale green eyes under their thin arched brows and smiled.

Evangeline introduced Molly as her favorite cousin, and I expected the usual fishy eye from the protective elder but instead got a friendly grin and a handshake that was firm. Obviously, she was one of those rare creatures who look and hope for the best from strangers.

She led us into her high-ceilinged kitchen, which had white cabinets all along the east wall, and made us sit down at a white enameled table for coffee and cookies.

I had told Evangeline that we'd ought to keep our errand vague and general, but she insisted everything had to be in the open. Molly was her best friend in the family and there wasn't to be any holding back.

Then she told her cousin I was a well-known private investigator who'd been hired by Mr. Brundage to find out about the accident that'd killed Alma's mother and others. She didn't mention that I'd begun it all working for the judge. Openness, I realized, had its limits—even among favorite relatives.

When I made noises about going to find a place to spend the night, Molly assured me I could stay at her neighbors.

"She's very reasonable and there's an outside stairway you can use if your work keeps you out late."

That was quickly settled, and Evangeline drove me downtown, dropped me off at the pile of rock they call City Hall, and I looked up Logan. As I settled into the chair beside his desk his bald partner came over to say hello and we even shook hands. The bald one's name was Flynn. They both talked about Baltz, the bootlegger hitman I'd clobbered with the toilet tank cover. They still thought that was awfully funny. After a while we got to my present errand and Logan lifted open hands.

"We got nothing. Checked everyplace. Like I say, he could be using an alias or maybe got a buddy he's bunking with."

I told him about the guys who'd trailed us from Toqueville.

"Got a license number?" asked Flynn.

"Yeah, but I can't claim they actually did anything to us."

"That's okay," he said, writing down the numbers I gave.

As he moved off, Logan explained they wouldn't try to pull them in. "We just want to spot the car and keep track, maybe find out where they're staying. That should lead us to your pigeon. This town's not too full of South Dakota plates."

That was probably something that'd occur to the gang, but on the other hand, it wasn't likely they'd expect me to be cozy with Minneapolis cops. I explained my plan to visit dance halls that night.

"You want some backup, right?"

"Well, I can't be sure there'll be any toilet covers handy if four guys move in on me."

He enjoyed that a little more than seemed called for and finally said I should hit the Marigold about ten. He and Flynn would be around.

"If there's no action there, we can move over to the Prom. That's outside our jurisdiction but I know the bouncer there and he won't be any problem."

I left City Hall about midafternoon and took in the wide, blue sky and the traffic noises. Big yellow streetcars made most of the racket, and watching them clatter by I thought I should take a ride, but the notion passed since I was to meet Evangeline in Dayton's bookstore for a ride back to Molly's.

I spotted my lady in the book department looking over a novel by Sinclair Lewis. There were several customers around, mostly women, and I thought she looked as smart as the best of them. When I told her that, she said I sounded like a guy making a pass at a stranger.

"How'd the police treat you?" she asked as she put the book back on its shelf.

"Fine," I said.

She looked skeptical but nodded politely and asked, "Okay, what's next?"

I said whatever she liked, and so we went around to see Minnehaha Falls but there wasn't enough water falling for any kind of a show. I could do better after two beers.

Then we drove back to Lake Calhoun, which had lots of water, parked in shade, and hiked along the shore, where folks were sitting around in bathing suits and a few actually made it into the water. There were kids hollering and couples snuggling and guys running around kicking sand on the innocent. Sunshine reflected on the blue water, which was barely ruffled by easy breezes.

It all put Evangeline in a dreamy mood, and we sat on grass under an elm a ways from the crowd. She told me she loved this town. It was exciting and beautiful and clean. I thought of asking if she'd ever seen pictures of the labor union battles in the streets, but it seemed a crummy thing to bring up so I forgot about it. I asked if she'd been here before, and she said yes, once when it was dark and rainy and she still loved it.

"The judge'll miss you," I said. "So will Annabelle."

"Let them move here."

"You think the judge would?"

She laughed. "What? And be a small frog in the big pool? He can't stand having one rival in Toqueville."

"What makes him that way?"

"Lots of things. He was youngest in a family of five. Sam was about eight years older than Cal and had three sisters between. They all bossed him around. Daddy was a star student and model son. Went to Yale and won honors. Uncle Cal had to settle for Brookings. That was more than any of the kids he grew up with ever managed, but he thought it was an awful comedown from Yale. For a while he thought about moving to Cranston when he was doing legal work there, but about then Daddy began to slow down and Uncle Cal got elected judge. What do you say we forget all that stuff and think of now? Have you see the Spanish houses around Lake of the Isles?"

I admitted I didn't remember them.

"They're beautiful. I don't suppose a man like you ever dreams of owning something grand?"

"Not much."

"But if you had a whole *lot* of money, what'd you do?"

I shook my head. She insisted I think about it, and finally I said maybe I'd buy a sailboat and head for the South Pacific.

"I'd like to find islands the missionaries never reached—if there are any."

"But you went to the Philippines and didn't stay."

"Well, I didn't say I'd go forever. I'd visit. Then try China, maybe."

"You'd stay a bum, that's what you'd do. Still roaming, just a rich bum."

She said that almost fondly, as though my awful failings were tolerable.

20

Molly served us chicken and dumplings for dinner. I took care of a leg, thigh, and wing, a load of mashed potatoes, a sample of green beans, and more than my share of the dumplings and watermelon pickles. Alma, I was happy to see, put away a fair share of groceries. I got Molly talking about Toqueville, which she had left a few years back but still had vivid memories of the town and its people.

"Winnie's mother, Sophie, was my best friend, you know. About everybody thought at first that she was nothing but Amos' shadow till he died, but that wasn't so at all. We met the first week she was in town. I was the church secretary then and she was already interested in women's suffrage but wasn't open about it because her husband got upset at the very mention. Before he got sick, according to Sophie, they had some grand battles on the subject, but he exploited his illness shamelessly and she was too kind to push him when she knew he didn't have much time left."

"She tell you about the business he'd been in?" I asked.

"Not much. Said he was in pharmaceuticals." She grinned impishly. "Actually, I think he started by mixing liquor with syrup in their kitchen and selling it on street corners and at fairs as a cure-all. Later on he had somebody making the stuff and hired men to sell for him.

167

Eventually, he was wholesaling it and may have finally sold what he called the 'formula' for it. Call it Amozon, based on his first name, you know."

"What was Sophie like?" I asked.

She laughed. "A little like the weather; changeable, unpredictable, impossible to ignore. She was tall and kind of bony but had delicate features and marvelous skin and hair. She came to our church, the Lutheran there in Cranston. Wore extravagant clothes, positively enormous hats, and said all sorts of startling, almost shocking things in the most casual way."

"Somebody told me she wasn't good-looking," I said.

"Really? I can't imagine who'd say such a thing."

"Judge Carlson."

"Ah," she said wisely, and didn't look at Evangeline. I did and saw her blush.

Molly started talking rapidly. She said that she and Sophie spent hours talking over coffee.

"Actually, she did most of the talking. She had incredible energy and passion. They built that wonderful house and Sophie was in charge of all the planning and furnishings. Made it like a palace. Then, when Amos died, she seemed to lose all interest in it. Turned all her attention to the suffragette movement, and I went along with her. She took charge of it all. Those were lively days, believe you me." She laughed sheepishly. "We thought we'd make a difference. If you listened to Sophie, you knew it would. Maybe it will, eventually."

She said that wistfully, then came to herself with a jerk and said well, it must be our little friend's bedtime. She looked surprised when I carried Alma to the bedroom and, after they had prepared her for bed, lay down with her.

"I'm all out of stories," I told Alma. "It's your turn."
She shook her head.

"Come on. Your ma told you some and I'll bet you remember. Tell me."

There was some stalling but finally she began. "Wanna ponsa time there was a prince. He lived inna castle and had to do ever-thing ennybody told 'um. He hadda eat what they said and wear stuff they put on him and do stuff just right and one day he tooka walk inna woods. He walked and walked and walked and got tired and fawdown. Anna nice old man picked 'um up and took him to a hut and gave him stuff to eat annelived happyeverafter."

"He liked the hut better than the castle?"

"Uh-huh."

"Why?"

"He din' hafta do ennything he din' wanna."

"Your mom told you that?"

She nodded.

I thought that over and decided about the worst thing I could do was take this small party back to the Wilcox Hotel and expose her to my ma.

When I came downstairs Evangeline was on her feet looking out the front window. "It's time we went to the dance," she told me, glancing at her watch. She gave me a look that laid it out plain we were going together.

On our way out to the car I told her this wasn't smart. "I won't have any trouble spotting Bo—I'm sure his gang will be with him, and if there's trouble, you'll just complicate things."

"All that has to happen," she told me, "is we find these people for your police friends and then they take over. And don't tell me you're going to handle this thing all by yourself because I know very well you're not crazy. At least not *that* crazy."

"So why're you coming?"

"Because you *might* be that crazy if I don't."

The Marigold Ballroom was bigger than most barns I could remember and held more people than Corden during the county fair. Right off it seemed unlikely I could find Boris Karloff dressed as the monster in all that mob, but after we danced a couple numbers and I'd circled the joint half a dozen times it didn't seem quite as hopeless.

I should admit I use the term "dance" pretty loosely. What I do is walk and hope I'm keeping the beat. Mostly it works okay if my partner doesn't try to teach me better or go off on her own.

Evangeline was fine. She looked around a little more than I liked and when we got a number slow enough for a bit of squeezing up, she gave me a dirty look and said cut that out.

I saw the cops, Logan and Flynn, on the fourth swing around. Logan was dancing with a blond floozy and Flynn was scowling at him. Logan thought that was very funny. He was a great laugher. The blonde looked bored.

When we hadn't sighted Bo or his friends by eleven I moved in on Logan and suggested we try the Prom. He wasn't too happy about leaving his blonde but reluctantly gave her up with a pat on the fanny and agreed to lead us to the midway between the Cities, where we'd find the Prom.

The drive lasted forever through nowhere; miles of flat town with one- and two-story buildings, all dead in the night.

The Prom didn't look like much from the outside, but

it had more floor space than the Marigold and there were booths beside the dance floor where you could sit, buy beer, and watch the action. The place didn't seem to have as many floozies; it was more a couples' joint. A big dude walked around the floor, I guessed him at two-and-a-half hundred and maybe six-three. He stalked couples who got too fancy and took up more than their share of the floor. Everywhere this guy moved couples parted like sheep before a wolf, and when he tapped a guy on the shoulder, he turned tame and shy.

Evangeline and I were doing my walk to a number that didn't fit when suddenly she stiffened as if I'd stepped on her.

"Bo!" she whispered.

I jerked my head around and saw only the giant bouncer moving toward a jitterbugging couple.

"He alone?" I asked.

"Darn!" she said, "I lost him. Just saw his face a second—he was looking right at me."

I moved us toward the wall, but we found no one we knew.

"I *know* it was him—and he recognized me, I'm sure."

"Great," I said, looking around, "now where's the cops when we need them?"

They were in a booth, swigging beer. I told them what Evangeline had seen. "If he's got us spotted," I said, "his boys can scout the cars outside and find ours."

Logan finished his beer, wiped his mouth, and slid out of the booth. "Okay, I'll drift out there like a sleepy drunk and get in our car. I can see yours from there. You follow after a minute and Flynn'll tail you from a ways back. We'd ought to pick up the whole gang by the time you get to your car."

We wandered a little as Logan headed for the door, and I kept an eye for any of the gang but none was in sight. A few seconds later I saw Flynn standing beside the big bouncer. He met my eye and nodded.

"Let's go," I told Evangeline.

She took my arm and walked close. We passed through the front door, turned right, and headed toward the lot. It was warm out and still. We passed the corner of the building without finding anyone in wait and I could feel some of the tension leave Evangeline.

"They've decided to run," she whispered.

I thought I saw a few necking couples in cars we passed but there was nothing threatening. We got to the Oldsmobile, I looked in front and back, and led us over to Logan's car.

He straightened up, looked around lazily, and said, "Seems like your girlfriend's been seeing things."

"I'm not his girlfriend," Evangeline told him icily, "and I know perfectly well what I saw. I haven't been swilling beer all night like some."

Logan got out and walked us back to our car. I saw Flynn with the bouncer watching from a ways off. Evangeline got into her car and slammed the door. Logan moved a few steps away after tipping his head toward his friends and I went along until he stopped and faced me.

"You're on a wild-goose chase, pal. And you're not going to get anywhere with that frozen frail."

"I've gone two hundred and fifty miles with her so far," I told him, "and I figure on doing it again."

"Sounds like a real thrill. So, you got any more bright

ideas on how Flynn and me can have an exciting Saturday night?"

"How about you tail us back to Minneapolis? Maybe we'll pick up something along the way."

"Why not? We're going back anyway."

Nothing happened. They followed us right up to the duplex, tapped the horn, and left. I walked Evangeline to the door. She was burning.

"I *did* see him."

"I never doubted it."

"You didn't back me up when you talked to that policeman."

"It wouldn't have impressed him."

"You could've said something so *I'd* know you didn't think I was a dimwit."

"I've never thought that."

"But you didn't let them know it because you were afraid they'd think you were besotted."

That was too true to argue. I told her not to worry about it.

"I'm not used to having people treat me as if I weren't around. I don't like those men. They think I'm a stupid kid. I could hear you talking—you think I'm deaf?"

Before I could answer, Molly opened the door.

"I'm sorry, dears," she said, "but Irene, my neighbor, where you're staying, she got a telephone call a bit ago and she's very upset. Some person asked for you, Mr. Wilcox. Asked that you call back. Irene wasn't expected to handle any telephone calls. I mean, she has that outside entrance so she doesn't have to be bothered once she goes to bed. You'll have to tell your friends you can't take calls there."

"I wasn't expecting any."

"Well, you can return it from here if you like."

I thanked her and we went inside. She led me to a telephone on a stand in the hall and handed me a slip of paper with a number. The women went into the kitchen and I could smell coffee as I called the operator. She rang the number I gave her, but no one answered.

"I don't understand it," said Molly. "Even if Irene got the number wrong, which wouldn't surprise me—I think she dies a little when she falls asleep—how'd anybody know you were staying over there? I didn't tell anyone."

"I don't figure it's any secret in Toqueville that Evangeline's got a cousin in Minneapolis," I said. "I've a notion that old Bo's gang keeps tabs on everything that'd be useful. The little routine we got driving here, followed by his buddies, seems to be part of a cat-and-mouse game he likes to play. Has he got any close family you ever heard of?"

"Bo?" She looked at Evangeline. "I think he was an only child. Do you know?"

"No. I think he came from under a rock."

"Winnie was an only child too, wasn't she?" I said.

Molly nodded. "What're you getting at?"

"I'm not real sure. I've got a notion that from one direction or another, Winnie could've been due to inherit. Either from her old man, or from her husband's family."

Molly folded her slim hands and rested her chin on them as she leaned her elbows on the kitchen table. "If Winnie was an heiress, now Alma is."

"Yeah."

"You think somebody figured to benefit by Winnie's death—that she was the target in that 'accident,' not Cody Jerome?"

"The idea's full of holes, but yeah, that's where I seem to be going."

"Then Alma could be in danger."

I admitted that could be.

"What should we do?" asked Evangeline.

"Get out of this place."

Just as Molly began to object we heard a gentle knock at the front door.

"Is the outside back door locked?" I asked Molly.

She nodded. "So's the outside front door to the porch. I locked it after you."

I slipped through the dark dining and living rooms, edged near the curtained door window, and snuck a peek through. There was no one in my limited view. The knock was not repeated.

Then I heard a knock from the rear. I went back on the double and met the women in the dining room. They had turned out the kitchen light.

"Was the knock on the inside door?" I asked.

"No," said Molly. "I'm going to call the police."

I agreed that was a good idea, but it didn't surprise me when she reported the line was dead.

"You got renters upstairs?" I asked.

"They're not home. Gone to Chicago for the World's Fair."

"Got a key?"

She said yes.

"Get Alma. You and Evangeline take her up there. Turn on the radio full volume and open the windows."

A thumping knock began at the front door. The women scrambled to get Alma, then snuck out the back door and upstairs.

I was near the back door when it thundered with

knocking. At least two men had to be at it. I closed the kitchen door, bolted it, and heard glass break in the middle bedroom, where Alma had been sleeping. I snatched a poker from the fireplace stand, raced to the bedroom, and saw a narrow jagged break in the window but no one around. I ran to the front door. There was a figure inside the porch, pounding on the door. I slipped the bolt, jerked the knob, and lunged, using the poker like a rapier. It had a hook instead of a point but it reached the pounder's throat. He squawked like a strangling cock just as the radio blared overhead.

I jumped back inside, slammed and bolted the door, and ran to check the middle bedroom as more glass broke. I swung the poker at the window, the upper pane shattered, there was an exclamation from outside, and a neighbor yelled, "Turn that goddamn radio down!"

"Call the cops, shithead," I yelled back.

I ran to Molly's radio, turned it on, and with a couple of twists found a blaring trumpet.

When I went to the back door and listened, there was no sound in the outside hall.

A quick tour of the apartment revealed no invaders and when I looked outside the yard appeared empty. I eased the kitchen door open, padded upstairs, and tapped a "Shave and a haircut, six bits" on the door. The floor creaked inside.

"It's Carl," I said. "I think our visitors left."

21

We didn't turn off the radios until the cops pulled up in front. They weren't convinced we were sober until they found the broken window in the bedroom and confirmed that our telephone line had been cut.

There was a big powwow in the kitchen deciding what to do about the rest of the night. Evangeline wanted us all to go downtown to a hotel, but Molly nixed that. She said we could go but she would stay in the house. She got her way.

The cops tailed us downtown to the Dykman Hotel, and on the way Evangeline whispered that we'd get a room together. I liked the notion but hoped the cops wouldn't go in with us, and they didn't. We signed in as Mr. and Mrs. Carlson, and nobody gave us a fishy eye because of course unmarried couples don't often show up with a four-year-old kid in tow.

They gave us a room with a double bed and a rollaway. Since Alma was naturally still wound up by all the excitement, I laid down with her on the double bed and told her how my ma had ridden in a covered wagon from New York State to South Dakota when she was only a year older than Alma. I described the rattlesnakes and buffalo they saw, and it might have been true but I don't remember Ma ever mentioning any critters. In fact, she didn't even talk about riding in the wagon. She said she remembered walking beside it but didn't explain why that'd be. A five-year-old kid couldn't add much burden to a wagon. Maybe she was born chunky, but even so . . .

Anyway, the little girl finally went to sleep and didn't wake when I moved her to the rollaway.

While all that had been going on Evangeline had changed into night clothes in the bathroom and came out wearing a quilted robe over a pink nightie. She'd brushed her hair and it was shiny smooth around her shoulders.

I tucked Alma in and looked around to see Evangeline sitting on the edge of the double bed with her arms folded tightly across her bosom. "You won't do anything, will you?" she said without looking at me.

"I didn't figure on sleeping in a chair or on the floor."

"I'm not suggesting that," she said with heat. We were both whispering.

I went into the bathroom and stared at my mug in the mirror over the sink while I ran cold water for a drink and rinse. The next step was dicey because I don't own a pair of pajamas, let alone a night shirt, and it didn't seem too bright to peel stark and move in with a woman who was already scared to death. It didn't seem much better to come out in my skivvies. Whiskers shaded my jaw enough so that I looked more like a bum than usual, but I figured if I tried shaving the lady would be convinced I had lustful plans, and while I did, it was pretty obvious it wouldn't pay to let her know it. I left the water running and took a leak sitting down while I thought about it all. It made me mad that I felt self-conscious about flushing the toilet, but of course I had to so she wouldn't get the notion I'd never used an indoor privy before.

I turned out the light and opened the door. The room was completely dark. I stood a moment, letting my eyes adjust, and pretty soon light leaking through the curtains showed the bed outline. I inched over to it, saw that Evangeline had taken the side away from the bathroom and was so near the edge she'd drop off if I so much as exhaled her way. I took off my duds, folded them on the chair, pulled back the covers, and crawled in.

For several seconds we lay there breathing. Then she said, "Don't be sore at me."

"I'm not."

She stirred a little and I guessed she'd turned on her back. That made something stir in me.

"You want to talk?" she asked.

"Okay."

"I won't be able to sleep," she said. Her face was turned toward me now and seemed close. "I'm afraid of those men, and of you, and that something awful's going to happen and nothing good can. You think Uncle Cal robbed Sophie Anderson, don't you?"

"That's not called robbery. Swindling, I think."

"And if you think that, you can also think he did something worse, like having Ellsworth killed because he knew about the swindle and might tell Brundage."

"I thought about that, yeah."

"Why do you think I came on this trip with you?"

"Not sure."

"You think maybe I came to seduce you out of exposing him, don't you?"

I admitted I'd thought of that, too.

"Would it work?"

I considered that.

"It wasn't an offer," she said.

"Oh."

"But Uncle Cal didn't do anything wrong. I mean, he

didn't swindle Winnie out of her inheritance or anything like that. He was very fond of her and her mother, too. I think maybe something went on between Sophia and Uncle Cal. That they were lovers once."

"He told me she was homely."

"Well, she wasn't exactly the sort of woman he always thought he wanted—you know—sweet and doll-like. Sophia sort of bowled him over with all her energy and positiveness. He resented that."

"Or maybe he was trying to slicker me."

"Maybe. But that wouldn't mean he'd done anything awful except adultery. He wouldn't want anybody to even *guess* that."

"I don't know. You can't hardly keep a secret like that in a town like Toqueville for long."

"But I don't think it went on for long—and remember, she lived in Cranston."

We were quiet a while. I heard Alma stir a couple times and guessed she was dreaming.

"Are we going back home tomorrow?" asked Evangeline.

"Yeah."

Alma began whimpering. After a couple moments I got up and went over to her bed. Suddenly, as I bent over, she jerked and cried out. The next moment she was sitting up.

"It's okay, Alma," I assured her, "you're okay."

She sat up, reaching for me. I picked her up and rocked her easy, telling her she'd only been dreaming.

"Bring her here," said Evangeline.

I did and put her between us and when Alma asked me to tell her about Cinderella I went through it. She made me fill in parts I skipped.

When she still wasn't sleepy I said she should tell me one of the stories her mother had told her, and after a short silence she began.

"Wanna ponsa time the little prince who ran away got big. And his daddy, the king, got old and went to look for him inna countryside and he came to where the prince was and asked to see all the young guys, only he was blind and couldn't see 'um but asked 'um to talk and touched their faces with his hands, and when he talked to the prince and touched him he alla sudden could see and took him back to the castle and everybody live happy-everafter."

"Holy cow," said Evangeline.

And we all went to sleep.

22

After breakfast in the hotel we picked up Molly and drove down to the police station and signed a complaint that no one figured would come to anything. Molly fed us lunch, and after a prolonged good-bye we took off for Toqueville.

I spent the first couple hours rubbernecking to see if we were being followed. We weren't. Alma was sleepy from her short night's rest, so I fixed her up with blankets on the floor of the back and she alternated between there and my lap in the front seat.

She quickly learned some of the more innocent kid songs I remembered and particularly liked—"The horses run around/Their feet are on the ground"; "Oh who will wind the clock while I'm away, away?"; "Run get the axe/There's a hair on baby's chin"; "And a boy's best friend is his mother, his mother."

When she finally tired out and went to sleep on the floor in back, Evangeline glanced my way. "I guess your friend Logan was right. This *was* a wild-goose chase and you didn't get anyplace with me."

"I crowded Bo into a move."

"You didn't prove anything. You just got us all in danger for nothing."

The only defense I could think of was that I hadn't

been the one who suggested bringing Alma along. That didn't strike me as a great argument.

"So what's your next bright move?" she asked.

"I'll check out records on the families involved. Who'd inherit what, if anything."

"You going to talk with Uncle Cal about that?" She kept her eyes on the road.

"I don't think I'll get much more from him. He isn't likely to know much about Ellsworth's family."

She made a tight mouth before speaking. "You don't trust him, do you?"

"Not a lot."

There was an awful lot of quiet in the car after that.

It was after six when we pulled off the highway and went into a small café for supper. Like most places of its kind, it had booths along one wall, a lunch counter opposite, and tables in the center. Four tables had been shoved together and a gang of guys, mostly in their fifties but a few younger, sat around drinking coffee. Seven of them were playing poker while the extras kibitzed. They were a hearty bunch, kidding and laughing but mostly proper. They wore overalls, high shoes, and blue work shirts.

Evangeline got a lot of quiet attention as we first came in. So did Alma. I got a couple glances and inspired some wonder, since it was obvious the lady hadn't picked me for my beauty and the kid showed no family resemblance to either of us. Once we settled down only the guys facing our booth kept looking, and even they tried to avoid being obvious.

They were the kind of guys I'd have liked to have around if Bo and his mob tried to move in.

Evangeline ordered beef roast, I had a hot pork sandwich, and Alma took a child's portion of chicken. Neither of my partners ever glanced at the men who quietly observed them.

While we waited for our orders Alma drank iced water and Evangeline sipped hot coffee now and then but mostly sat with a slender finger hooked through the cup handle, and kept frowning. Finally, she looked up at me. "I keep wondering what you're thinking," she said.

"You probably know."

She blushed a little, shook her head, and glanced at Alma. "I mean about Uncle Cal."

"That's what I meant."

She blushed some more, lifted her head, and said, "Okay, I asked for that. But do you really believe that my father and Uncle Cal did Winnie and her mother out of their money? That's why Brundage hired you, isn't it? To dig that up and disgrace them."

"He just hired me to check out Ellsworth. Neither one of us spelled out what that'd bring out."

"Things like that don't happen in Toqueville. Everybody knows each other too well."

"That's just why such things *do* happen. In small towns all the law's in about three heads and the citizens just naturally trust those in charge and don't worry if strangers or weird types get shafted a little or a lot. All these crazy folks look out for each other and if somebody blows a whistle, especially somebody from outside, they close ranks and keep him out. Even if I could prove the judge was a crook and got Brundage to back me up, the townsfolk'd be against me because he was *their* crook.

They wouldn't stand for some outsider to come in messing with their nice comfortable system."

"My father would absolutely *never* cheat widows or orphans, and neither would my uncle. He's no saint, but he's not the devil, either."

"Okay. But look at it another way. Say both of these guys figured Sophia wasn't responsible. That she was going to waste the money left to her. You think it's impossible that they would decide to get it out of her hands and keep it for the daughter? You think either one of those guys believed in women's suffrage?"

She fiddled with the cup and admitted no, it wasn't likely.

"And the judge took Winnie in when it was obvious her husband wasn't going to take care of her or the kid."

Our food was delivered and we got at it. Evangeline chewed her beef so delicately I couldn't believe she'd ever get it to where she could swallow, but finally she polished it off. By then Alma'd had all the chicken she cared for and the two of them took off for the ladies'. Just before they reached the door, Alma peeked back and waved as if she thought I needed reassurance.

A little later we were chasing the sun toward the horizon. It paused at the rim, just a little south of where the yellow road divided the brown prairie before us. Evangeline squinted and shaded her eyes with her left hand until the sun sank from view, and darkness edged in.

Aquatown looked lively as a cemetery but a little better lit as we skirted its edge and headed into the home stretch. I kept an eye on sidestreets and parked cars. Just before we hit the city limits west of town, I spotted a dark

car in a closed gas station drive and thought I could see
two men inside. Despite poor light, I was sure it wasn't
Mac's black Buick.

I twisted around as we passed and saw it come to life
and move onto the highway behind us. The lights didn't
come on until it was within three car lengths of us.

Evangeline's head jerked at the sudden light. "Where'd
that come from?" she demanded.

"He was waiting in a gas station a ways back."

"Oh, Lord."

"I only saw two guys in it."

"You think it's not them?" she said, glancing at me
hopefully.

"Either that or they've split up. It's not the Buick.
May be Bo's Graham Paige."

She leaned forward, pressing down on the accelerator
while alternately watching the road ahead and the mirror.

I peered over the seatback trying to see if Alma had
awakened, but it was too dark. She seemed to be still.

I turned to Evangeline. "Maybe we'd better circle
back to town."

"I'm going home."

"They've got two cars and a plan. I don't think that
gives us good odds. In about two minutes you'll top the
rise before the slough and I've got a hunch that's where
things'll happen."

She concentrated on the road ahead. I wished I could
shove her out of the driver's seat and take over but it
wasn't practical at the moment and what was worse, I
guessed she was at least as good a driver as I was.

The car behind stayed half a block back.

"Crawl in back and wrap yourself around Alma," said
Evangeline. "You can't help me here."

It seemed a milktoast thing to do but it also made sense, so over the back I went, being careful not to land on Alma. I didn't touch her at first, just sat in the corner, looking forward then back as we reached the hill crest and started down. There were no barriers in sight. Evangeline floored the gas pedal.

"There's a sharp left half a mile ahead," I warned her.

She let me know she was aware of that.

As we sighted the curve warning she eased on the brake. I felt the car's rear drift and heard gravel rattling, but she pulled it out nicely. The car behind began to gain.

She tapped the brake again, but our speed hardly changed.

I looked around the bend. It wasn't dark enough out to hide the car straddling the road and still another car backed at an angle into the shallow ditch facing us with its light high from the slope.

Evangeline hit the curve going fast, started a skid, swung the steering wheel to match the slide, slowed a lick, hit the gas once more, down-shifted to second, and spun the steering wheel back left. We about-faced, shot back toward the curve, saw the trailing car go skidding into the ditch, and, to my horror, Evangeline pulled the same maneuver again. While we'd been spinning, the car in the ditch came digging out, skidded, overcompensated, and headed for the opposite ditch as we shot past, swerved around the parked car astraddle the road, and streaked toward the second curve. We went around it in a beautifully controlled skid that brought us to the absolute edge of the ditch and seemed to hang there for a week before Evangeline hit the gas again.

Suddenly we were on the straight road in high gear,

roaring on at ninety miles an hour. I was muttering "Jesus Christ" in a tone of total respect as Alma stirred and lifted her head.

"What?" she asked.

"Everything's fine, honey," I assured her. "You're in the hands of God, or at least an angel. Go to sleep."

23

I asked Evangeline as we approached Toqueville where in hell Cody Jerome learned how to teach her driving like that. She said he'd been taught to drive by a friend who worked for bootleggers in Minneapolis.

"And you wouldn't make love with him?"

"No."

It seemed to me that was the least she could have done but guessed she wouldn't take that well and kept quiet.

"You all think alike, don't you?" she said, glancing at me.

"I was kidding," I lied.

"No you weren't. You think I owe him. Well, he didn't teach me anything for my benefit. All he was after was getting me bare in the back seat, and that doesn't make me owe him anything. I never made any bargains."

She drove straight to her uncle's house and charged into the living room to tell him all that'd happened. I took Alma upstairs and put her to bed. For once she was knocked out enough so there was no need for a story, and I hustled back down to the living room.

Evangeline was still talking and the judge was listening very thoughtfully. His pale blue eyes moved from her face to mine and back with no more expression than as if she'd been describing a movie or a dream. Her anger grew as she spoke, and when she finished with the business about the cars she asked with some steam what he was going to do about all of that.

"What do you think I should do?" he asked calmly.

"I think you should call Al Jacobsen and Tom Purvis and see to it that those hoodlums are thrown in jail and then just take it from there."

"All right. But first, let's look at a few of the facts—do you mind?"

"Like what?"

"Did you see any of those men clearly, at the dance hall, around Molly's house, or on the highway?"

"I saw Bo—"

"Across a very large ballroom, for a fleeting second, isn't that what you told me?"

"It was more than a second and it wasn't that far."

"But it wasn't long and it wasn't close. How good was the light?"

"It was," she said coldly, "sufficient."

"My dear, I'm not trying to make you sound foolish, I'm only trying to make you aware of how weak your case is. You, Wilcox, did you see the man in the dance hall?"

I admitted I hadn't.

"Did you recognize anyone around the house when it was besieged?"

"I think I hit Fisher when I caught him at the door, but it was darker than hell."

"You never saw anyone you could identify in the cars, did you?"

I hadn't.

"You got no license numbers. You couldn't identify, positively, any of the cars, right?"

"Come on!" cried Evangeline. "Whose side are you on?"

"I'm on your side, but I can't help you by encouraging the sort of unsubstantiated charges you're making."

"We saw them in the café yesterday. And the people there, they'll remember them."

"What if they do? From what you told me, those three fellows walked in, sat down, drank coffee, and went out. Did they threaten you? Even speak to you?"

"Well, what were they doing there, if not threatening us?"

"They'll undoubtedly claim they were driving to Minneapolis and just happened on you."

Evangeline glared at me as if all this was my fault and the judge gave me his calm gaze, still keeping his judicial expression.

I leaned back in the couch and began rolling a smoke. "Judge, I sure wish I'd met more lawmen like you in my time. Anytime folks accused me of anything at all, no cop or judge ever questioned 'em a second. I just got hauled in and worked over. You think maybe you could ask Al to find out if anybody found a car abandoned on the road we just came in on? And could you get Purvis to sort of check up on his traveling citizens? See if they're home or if they show up pretty soon?"

He gave me a look that didn't carry any gratitude I could recognize but thanked me solemnly and got out of his chair with a grunt. We watched him walk heavily to the telephone on its stand in the corner and jiggle the hook. "Get me Al Jacobsen," he told the operator.

While he was on the phone, Evangeline went into the kitchen and started heating water in a percolator. I stood by the door, watching as she measured coffee into the strainer while taking in the judge's monologue. He delivered the story in deliberate, deadpan style, then hung up and went back to his easy chair.

Evangeline put the coffee can back under the counter and got cups out of the cupboard, moving with a deliberation that matched the judge's talk to the cop.

"What'd you expect him to do?" I asked.

"I thought he'd get mad and raise Cain."

"That's not judicial."

"I thought he cared about me."

"Maybe he never figured *you* were in danger."

She put down the last cup and stared at me. The percolator burped and splashed water up into the glass top of its cover.

"What're you saying?"

"He figures they were trying to stop the car to get at me. Not you."

She sat down in the chair nearest the kitchen table. I thought some of the anger had left her face. Her head turned to glance at the percolator. Then she faced me again.

"You actually think he wants you killed so you can't expose him for robbing Sophia and Winnie of their inheritance?"

The floor creaked behind me and I turned to see the judge standing in the hall. He walked slowly past me into the kitchen, pulled out a chair opposite Evangeline, and sat down.

"My dear," he said, "can you believe I'd ever condone anything that could possibly cause you harm?"

She stared at him levelly. "You might. If you could convince yourself it was for the common good. How much money was involved when you handled the Anderson place?"

"A trifle over twenty-five thousand dollars. And I'll tell you exactly what I did. I persuaded Sophia to put it in a trust for Winnie, with monthly payments to begin when Winnie reached twenty-five. It would've taken care of her comfortably through Alma's early years."

"Was Winnie pregnant when you set that up?" asked Evangeline.

"We didn't know. But it seemed rather inevitable. It was apparent early on that she was promiscuous."

"How'd you persuade Sophia?"

"That wasn't difficult. She was a good-hearted woman, for all of her abrasiveness, and she had supporters of her work and no great need for money otherwise. In her last years I doubt she ever bought or prepared a meal for herself. People like your cousin Molly provided."

"You fed her some yourself, didn't you, Judge?" I asked.

He ignored me and kept his eyes on his niece.

"Has Bo Grummen ever worked for you?" she asked.

"Never. He's a maniac. And a man like Wilcox makes him murderous. Just the fact that Wilcox has the gall to challenge or threaten him at all is enough to make him try and kill him. Anyone in town can tell you that."

They were sitting there watching each other when I finally said it looked like the coffee was done. Evangeline jumped up and turned off the gas as the telephone rang.

"That's most likely Al," the judge told me. "You want to get it?"

I did.

"You can tell the judge," said Al, "the highway patrol

hauled a Hudson from across the highway on the jog west of Aquatown. It was stolen from a fellow staying at the Bjornson Hotel yesterday evening. He hadn't even missed it yet. You get a look at the guys trying to bushwhack you?"

"No. We were always looking into their headlights."

"Uh-huh. What happened in Minneapolis?"

I told him.

"Can you and Tom Purvis pull those guys in and check them out?" I asked. "See if Fisher hasn't got a good bruise on his neck where I caught him with a poker."

"You want to sign a complaint?"

"The judge doesn't think it'll stick, but I'll do anything that'll get those guys answering some questions."

"If they come back."

"Oh, they'll be back, all right. I figure they'll be at their jobs in the morning like nothing'd happened. And Bo'll be working on the highway."

"Well," said Al, "I tried calling Tom but nobody answered at the hall. I suppose he's out around the town somewheres."

I thought he might even have gone home but didn't say so because I figured Al wouldn't admit the possibility, let alone test it.

"Has Cody Jerome's car ever been brought back to town?" I asked.

"Yeah, as a matter of fact I went over Saturday morning with Chuck Compton and got it. Why'd you ask?"

"I thought maybe Cody'd loan it to me."

"He'd more'n likely rent it. Cody don't pass up any chances for a dime."

I thanked him and went back to tell Evangeline and the

judge what had happened. I turned down coffee and said I was going to bed. Evangeline said she'd walk a ways with me. The judge frowned but kept still.

It was a little after ten when we stepped outside. There was no moon but stars were out strong and the Milky Way sparkled a path across the black sky. Even the Little Dipper was in plain sight and the air was still. Someone laughed on a porch we passed and the only other sound was the hum of crickets.

"What'd you and the judge talk about while I was on the phone?" I asked.

"You."

"Tell me about it."

"He wanted to know what happened between you and me in Minneapolis. I told him just how it was. I don't know if he believed me or not. I told him you'd been a gentleman. That you respect other people's feelings and rights and don't take advantage."

"I can see why he might not believe you."

She laughed and took my arm. "I exaggerated, I know. But there's *some* truth in it. You aren't anything like as tough as you pretend."

I pulled her a little closer as we walked and she smiled at me.

"What made you ask him if he'd hired Bo?" I asked.

The smile faded some. "I knew you suspected it. I just decided to bring it out into the open."

"You didn't maybe want to let him know I'd guessed that?"

She came to a halt and jerked me around to face her. "Would you be thinking things like that if I'd let you make love to me?"

"I might."

"If I was on their side, why'd I have gotten us out of that trap on the highway?"

"I don't figure you're on Bo's side. You just didn't know what the whole business was about, but now you're beginning to guess and you aren't anxious to land the judge in the soup. What the hell, he's your uncle and the closest thing you got to a daddy."

"I don't *need* a daddy!"

"No, I don't guess you do."

"You didn't believe him about the trust, did you?"

"Oh, that's probably true enough. But I figure he also made arrangements so he got his share or a touch more. I think he had Sophia royally hornswoggled. People like her, ones with a mission, get out of touch with practical things sometimes. And she'd been used to letting men handle the money. I think your uncle and your pa were smart enough to strip her clean and not worry, so long as she was taken care of while she lived and there'd be something for the daughter and grandchild. He did take care of them, didn't he? Who'd question him even if it did get him a housekeeper?"

"I think you're awful."

"What you think is, I'm right."

She said, "Never!" and humphed off.

24

Simpson said he still didn't have the glass for my Model T when I went around to his garage after breakfast. It made me mad because I couldn't believe it was that big a problem. I jawed at him some without making any impression, and a little after noon managed to get Cody Jerome on the telephone and reminded him how willing he'd said he was to help out. He said he remembered fine, what'd I want, and I said his car for a few days.

There was just a long enough pause to make me think he was going to weasel out, but then he said of course, absolutely, he'd be delighted but he didn't have the key. I said that was no problem, Al had it.

That put another pause in the dialogue before he asked how was Alma and had I made progress with Evangeline. I passed both subjects over easy and gave him some more silence. Finally, he wanted to know had I met Bo yet.

I said no, but it wasn't for lack of trying. Somehow the tough guy had turned out to be shy.

"My friend," he said with wonderful warmth, "Bo is a lot of things but shy is not one of them. Take my word for it, that is one son of a bitch you don't want to tangle with. He will kill you."

"Well," I said, "I'll try to keep your car from getting wrecked."

He didn't seem to be particularly comforted by that assurance.

Half an hour later I had the keys and climbed into the car, a green-and-black Chevy four-door with clean upholstery, little handles on the door posts for folks to grab for getting in and out, and flower holders on the upper back sides near the window. It purred just fine and I wheeled it the twenty miles to Cranston, drove straight to Bo's house, hiked up to the front door, and knocked.

After a few seconds steps came up from below and the inner door opened slowly. A tawny face framed by dark curls appeared behind the screen, which veiled her so I saw little more than white teeth and dark eyes peering at me. "Yah?" she said softly.

"Sarah? I'm looking for Bo."

"Who're you?"

I told her.

The dark head shook. "He's not here."

"Go back to work on the highway?"

"Uh-huh."

"I hear you got married."

She nodded and I saw the white teeth again.

"Where?"

"Last week."

"Yeah, but where? In Minneapolis?"

"I'm not s'posed to talk to you."

"Why not?"

"You're bad."

"Bo tell you that?"

"I'm gonna close the door now," she said, but moved it only a little.

"I figured you'd be taller," I said.

She giggled. "I thought you would be, too."

I grinned. "You think I'd be a blond?"

"No. They said you was part black."

"Which part?"

She giggled again.

"Have a good time in Minneapolis?" I asked.

"Uh-huh."

"Stay in a hotel?"

"Stayed at the Lincoln," she said proudly. "Room had two beds and a big bathroom was all ours and a young fella in a uniform brought us breakfast, right there in the room."

"I bet you got new clothes, too."

"Sure did. A white dress with a big bow at the waist and a littler one up by the collar and shoes to match with white bows. I got married in all that."

"And I bet you got a nightie?"

"You *are* bad," she said, tilting her head.

"I guess Bo treats you pretty fine, huh?"

"Sometimes." A little of the lilt went out of her voice. I wished I weren't looking at her through the screen.

"See a lot of Bo's friends while in Minneapolis?"

She drew back. "I'm not s'posed to talk to you. Good-bye."

"Will he be back tonight?" I asked, but the door closed and latched firmly. I stood a second, listening. There wasn't a sound from behind the door, so I turned and left.

Purvis showed no signs of being tickled when I found him sitting at his desk in City Hall. I asked if he'd talked with Al Jacobsen and he said yes.

"Talked with Bo's guys yet?"

"Uh-huh. They admit they were with him last night

but claim they spent all afternoon and evening at his place. Playing cards."

"Old Maid, I suppose."

"I never asked."

I looked at him a while and he looked back without embarrassment. I started out.

"You going to talk with them?" he asked.

"Yeah."

"I'll come along."

The wind was up and dust whipped along Main Street, making us squint and scowl and keep our mouths shut. We ducked into the bakery, which felt hot and smelled sweet. The fat lady greeted 'us like customers and said yes, Arlo was out back. We found him sitting on stacked flour bags that he'd evidently just brought in from a truck in the alley. He had flour dust all over his skivvy shirt and bare arms which rested on his knees as he bent over with a cigarette dangling from his mouth. He looked up as I stopped in front of him but didn't raise his head.

I squatted and looked at his neck. The bruise under the scuffed skin surface was a combination of purple and sick yellow.

"Had an accident?" I asked.

He took the cigarette from his mouth, let smoke drift out, and blinked as it floated past his eyes. "Ran into a low branch last night."

"Uh-huh. Running through the woods, I suppose."

"That's right."

"That before or after you played poker at Bo's?"

He took a drag on his cigarette, squinted against his exhale, and said, "After."

"Somebody catch you cheating?"

"I was chasing a gal."

"Who?"

"That'd be telling."

"You must not have caught her."

He grinned. "She caught me."

"Lucky for her. And lucky the branch wasn't a couple feet lower."

"Sure was."

"You were seen by people besides Evangeline and me back at the café Saturday," I told him.

"That was Saturday. I never said I was at Bo's then."

"Why were you guys following us?"

"We weren't. Just took a ride."

"To visit the girl you were chasing Sunday night?"

"Who knows?"

"So you were back in Toqueville Saturday night?"

"By golly, you got all the answers. Why you keep asking questions?"

"Sometimes I wonder."

I got up and walked out. Purvis trailed along. We ducked our heads against the wind and moved toward the creamery.

"What'd you think of all that?" I asked Purvis.

"I think you got yourself a problem nailing any of these boys. They're gonna stick together no matter."

"You think maybe Tucker's the simplest of the crowd?"

He glanced at me. "Yeah, I guess so."

"Okay. I'm going to work on splitting them up. Don't cross me, okay?"

"Depends on how you go about it."

"Just hold back a while, okay?"

He looked bothered but didn't say no.

Tucker was unloading milk cans from a farmer's truck

when we got to the creamery. He handled them smooth and easy but each time he made the lift his lip curled, showing the gap in his front teeth. He ignored us until he had all the cans inside, then hitched up his pants and gave Purvis an innocent look.

Purvis looked at me. I stared at Tucker. Finally, he twitched and glanced my way.

"I saw you in Bo's car last night," I told him.

His head jerked. "The hell you did."

"Evangeline saw you, too."

"She couldn't."

"Oh yes—the light wasn't in our eyes all the time, not when we did the spin."

He shook his head violently.

"And Arlo's admitted you were there."

His jaw sagged and he scowled. "Yeah? So where was he?"

"In Mac's Buick. It was you and Bo in the Graham Paige, Fisher and Mac in the Buick."

His eyes flickered toward Purvis, who stared hard and slowly nodded. Tucker shook his head again. "Go on, why'd Arlo tell you anything?"

"He talked," I said, "because he's too smart to take the rap for Bo. Because this whole business that started off easy turned out tough when you guys murdered a woman and two kids. You thought you were just giving Cody a hard time because he owed Bo, but it turned out to be murder. And what the hell was there in it for you, or Arlo, or Mac? I mean, it's not as if you guys were all in on killing Ellsworth. Bo handled that all by himself, didn't he? Maybe he didn't even tell you at all."

Tucker turned toward Purvis with open hands. "What's this guy talking about? He's crazy—"

"I think," said Purvis, "we'd best go over to City Hall and talk some."

"I don't wanna go to City Hall, I wanna talk to Arlo—"

Purvis shook his head. "Who you're going to talk to is me. Let's go."

Tucker started to shake his head, but Purvis brought his right hand down to the butt of the gun on his hip, and after a little more sputtering, Tucker became abject and walked between us out to the street and east to City Hall.

I was glad the street was deserted as we made the short hike and suggested to Purvis when we got inside that he park our man in the cell while I made a couple telephone calls. He went along with that and as soon as we were alone asked who I was going to call.

"I just wanted to talk with you. Give me a little time with him alone. I won't touch him. Just let me sit outside that cell and talk to him a while. See what I can do."

"What you said there in the creamery, was that true? Did you and Evie see him?"

"Did Arlo tell us anything?" I asked.

He stared at me a moment, sighed, and said, "Okay. The way he reacted, I think you guessed right. It shook him when you said how they were split."

"I figured Bo wouldn't want Tucker off on his own any way, any time. He probably figures Arlo's smart and tough enough to work on his own, and Mac about the same. What I want to do is make Tucker realize that he's in big trouble and that Bo would turn on him like a terrier on a rat if he gets the notion we've even been talking with him."

"All right. I'll give you half an hour. But I'll be listening."

"Fine."

I went back to the cell. Tucker was sitting on the bunk, hunched over, rubbing his big hands together as if trying to get them warm.

"You were followed by Minneapolis cops when you were in town there," I told him. "We gave them Mac's license number and they tailed you when you met Bo. They just laid back when you were banging on the house and didn't move till I gave them the signal with the radio. They slipped up on tailing you away, but they'll back us up on you being there. Purvis is talking to the cop in Minneapolis right now."

" 'At's all bullshit," said Tucker.

I sat down on the floor, rolled a smoke, and offered him one. He suggested I stick it in an unlikely place. I said no thanks, lit up, and hugged my knees.

"You ever wonder why so many guys killed themselves in jail cells?" I asked.

He stared at me.

"I mean, there's gotta be a reason that happens so often. I been in a lot of cells. I know. You ever been in one before?"

He shook his head.

"You feel like a damned canary, don't you? Think about it. You know why they say convicts sing when they spill the beans? Follows, right? In a cage, like a canary. But that's not the tough part. It's when late at night they come around to talk to you. One of the things they do is they take handcuffs and cuff you to the bars. See that cross bar up there, near the top? They cuff you to that one. Your toes won't touch the floor. You can't believe how heavy a man gets hanging by his wrists. Then they cuff your ankles to bars below. That's to keep you from jerking up your knees when they hit you in the balls. In some jails they just beat the hell out of you with wide leather belts. They don't leave much of a mark unless they keep it up too long, but it gets your attention real good. Some guys just like to squeeze your balls. It's sickening, you know? What kind of a fruitcake'd get a kick out of squeezing a man's balls?"

"You're trying to scare me."

"You're damned right. I don't want any man to go through that stuff. What you've got to get through your thick skull is, it can happen to you."

"Purvis wouldn't do anything like that."

"You could be right, I don't know the man that well. But your problem is, you'll get moved to Toqueville. That's where the trial'll be because that's where the folks killed came from. The guy asking you questions'll be Al Jacobsen. Him and his boys. And none of them remember you as a kid or know any of your relatives or care how fine you played football for good old Cranston High. To them you'll just be that asshole from Cranston who murdered a girl and two kids they watched grow up. And the jury'll be folks that knew those people. Hell, it may never get to a jury, they might drag you out of the jail and hang you on the nearest elm."

"But dammit, I never killed anybody! I was just along with the guys and we followed them a while and that dumb kid driving the Dodge went nuts and missed the turn. That's all."

"That's all? What kind of a moron are you? You guys chased them, banged into the rear end of their car, probably forced them off the road—"

"No we didn't either! We just crowded them some to scare old Cody and that dumb kid panicked."

"Doesn't make any difference what you planned or that you weren't driving the car and didn't mean any harm. You were with them. That makes you an accessory and they've got you by the balls, Tuck. It doesn't matter a damn it was Bo's fault, you three stooges are in it up to your necks. That's the way the law goes."

Tucker offered a number of observations about the law, none of them kind or seemly, and I nodded in perfect agreement. And let him know how helpful his comments would be to his case.

"The fact is," I told him when he'd shut up, "you can get out of this whole thing clean as a whistle. So can Mac, if he's smart. Bo's the guy at the bottom of it all and he's the guy to take the fall. You know damned well he killed Ellsworth for Cody Jerome, so old Cody could come into the family by marrying Winnie."

He wouldn't meet my eyes and finally said he'd have to talk to Mac before he said anything more.

I went back to Purvis and we talked it over. I suggested we move Tucker to Toqueville and pick up Mac so we could work on him a while. He said no, we'd stick Tucker in a spare room upstairs and question Mac with Tucker handy, which would also save trouble with a lawyer when Tucker got one.

I was awed by all the concern for legal proprieties in Cranston. I'd never seen such delicate concerns for a prisoner by cops who'd arrested me over the years. Most of them made up their law as they went along.

Tucker was moved and a deputy was assigned to keep an eye on the door while Purvis went to pick up Mac. I waited in his office.

Mac came in with the cop looking more amused than disturbed and didn't change any even when Purvis locked him in the cell. He grinned at Purvis and asked him what the hell he thought he was doing.

Purvis tilted his head my way and walked back to his office.

I took out my fixings, rolled a smoke, and offered it to Mac. He said, "Why not?" accepted it and a light, and watched as I rolled another for myself.

"You a deputy now?" he asked me.

"No, just a guy with friends. Like you, in a way. Only none of my friends have killed anybody lately. What I'm trying to do is straighten out a few details in this business you and the other two stooges and Bo have been up to. I know where he is. What I can't figure out is why you guys are tagging along like dumb sheep."

He puffed on his cigarette, leaned back on the bunk, and squinted at me. "What business you talking about?"

"Murder, mostly. I could see you going along with hassling me just for laughs, but killing a helpless drunk and then running two kids and a girl to death, that's something else."

He watched me calmly. "How much Irish you got?"

"Almost half."

"Green or orange?"

"Orange."

"That figures."

I let that stand while I watched him. "I was explaining to Tucker a while ago," I said, "about being an accessory. He's not the brightest guy I've met, but he caught on pretty quick."

Mac looked at his cigarette, which was already half gone. "Oh," he said, "you been talking to Tuck?"

"Mostly I was listening to him."

"Yeah?" He met my eyes and tried to grin, but it didn't take. His face was stiff.

"He's not too crazy about Bo, you know," I said.

He didn't comment on that.

"I figure Bo's let him know he's not too bright."

Mac dropped his cigarette on the floor and stepped on it carefully.

"He's got a lot of respect for you, though," I said. "I mean Tucker."

He looked past me and said Tuck was all right.

"Yeah. He's not too proud of killing the girl and the two kids."

That brought a murderous scowl. "Tuck didn't kill them. None of us did. That was just a plain accident."

"It was a plain murder. Maybe you guys *were* just trying to scare Cody. But what you figured on and what happened were two different things and all the law takes on is what happened, not what some bloody bastard and his three stooges planned. Arlo and Tuck aren't going to take murder raps just to show Bo they love him. Sooner or later, those two guys are gonna sing and get off and all the charges'll land on you and Bo. Purvis has got enough to make his case right now, but I'm talking to you because we think you're smarter than Tuck and would make a better witness. And between us Irishmen, I don't like the idea of you taking the fall with Bo when I know damned well it was all his doing and he's making all the gravy."

I went on to tell him I knew he'd been with Fisher the night before when the four of them had tried to bushwhack Evangeline and me. "I suppose that was another case of just trying to scare somebody? Or did you really plan to kill us and that little girl?"

He tried to deny having anything to do with that, but I ran over him with what I'd confirmed with Tuck and could see it shook him. Still, he didn't spill anything.

I reported to Purvis and after some discussion he agreed to call Judge Carlson.

The judge took in my report and agreed we should pick up Bo and Arlo and deliver them to cells in Aquatown. He'd call there to clear things and also said he'd send Al over to pick up Mac.

Purvis, his deputy, and I drove out to where Bo was supposed to be working on the highway only to learn he hadn't shown up. So we came back and went to his house.

Sarah answered the door. She said she couldn't let us in and Purvis told her she had no choice in the matter and when she tried to close the door against him he moved in quick and a moment later we were down in the basement living room.

I noticed right away that Sarah kept her face turned but was too busy looking for Bo at first to pay any mind. A quick search of the three rooms showed us the man wasn't around and we all gathered in the living room. Sarah kept holding her right hand up to her cheek and eye, which of course made us stare, and finally, looking defiant, she jerked it down and held her head high. Her cheek was purple and swelling half-closed one bright blue eye. Then I saw the bruise on her bare forearm.

"Bo do that?" asked Purvis.

"I slipped in the tub and hurt myself," she said primly.

"Uh-huh. And he helped you up so hard you still got his finger marks on your arm. He's rough, isn't he?"

She turned her face so we only looked at the good side. Her skin was smooth and pale. I guessed she couldn't be twenty. She stared at Purvis a moment with her good eye, glanced at the deputy, and then me. Purvis asked where Bo was.

"Working," she said while staring at me.

"No he's not," said Purvis. "We just came from there and he hasn't shown up."

She shrugged.

"He's in big trouble, Sarah. It'd be for his own good you tell us where he is."

"I can't tell you where he is when I don't know, can I?"

"You probably got some idea. You married him, didn't you?"

"Marryin' a man don't make you know all about him."

"Did he tell you to flirt with Cody Jerome at the dance last week?" I asked.

Her blue eyes narrowed on me and her head turned a little. "Why'd he do that?"

"To start a fight."

"He said it was okay if I danced with him."

"You're saying Cody tried for you and before you said yes you checked with Bo?"

"Of course."

I grinned at her. "You're a girl who knows how to handle a man, don't you?"

I got a little smile in return. "Sometimes. But I got this," she said, raising her face, "thanks to you."

"Tuck tells us you were in the car that followed Cody and the Hendricksons that night," said Purvis.

Her face stiffened and her lower lip stuck out. "I don't believe it. Tuck'd never say anything like that about me."

"Why not?" I asked.

"Because he's in love with me. Besides, I wasn't there, I didn't go with 'em."

"Where'd they leave you?"

"At Miller's bar."

"How long'd you wait there?"

"I don't know. I fell asleep."

"He tell you what happened when he got back?"

She thought about the question. The three of us watched her. Then she looked squarely at me. "Tuck never said I was in that car, did he?"

I shook my head. "He was your fella before Bo moved in, wasn't he?"

She looked away and nodded.

"Tuck never hit you, did he?" I asked.

She shook her head.

"How come you married Bo, Sarah?"

She sighed. "Didn't seem to have a choice. He wanted I should and everybody does what Bo wants. They don't, there's big trouble."

"Not after this," I said. "You give us a little help and he won't ever smack you around again. And you can help Tuck out of trouble, too. You don't and Tuck'll go to jail as long as Bo. You've got that figured out, haven't you?"

She held out a little longer, but not much. When she started crying, the deputy grinned and I wanted to slug him. Purvis just looked sorrowful.

When she finally agreed to go with us I told her to put a nightie and anything else she needed in a bag. She went into the other room.

Purvis and I held a quick, quiet powwow. I suggested he take her and Tucker to Aquatown for safekeeping until we ran down Bo.

"It might even help if you put the couple in the back seat and let'em talk," I told him.

"They might just build up their own story."

"I don't think so. They both got reason to hate Bo. I think they'll end up sticking it to him for all they're worth."

In the end, after a talk with Al Jacobsen by telephone, Purvis agreed.

25

After Purvis and his deputy left with our canaries I went back to Doc Leigh's place and was talking in the kitchen with Annabelle when Evangeline showed up.

"Where's Alma?" she asked.

"Why ask me?" demanded Annabelle. "You had her last."

"She was out in the sandbox," said Evangeline. "I went in to get some iced tea and when I came back, she was gone. I thought she'd come over here."

They both looked at me as I got up.

"We'll look around," I said.

"Oh no—" said Annabelle, "you don't think—"

"We'll look around."

She wasn't anywhere we looked.

The two women started going house to house. I went inside and headed for the telephone when it rang.

"Wilcox?" said a familiar voice.

"Yeah."

"This is Arlo Fisher."

"I was just going to call you."

"So I saved you the trouble. Still looking for Bo?"

"Yeah."

"Fine. I know where he is."

"So tell me."

"You do it alone, understand?"

"Right."

"You alone now?"

"Yeah."

"Okay. Get this straight the first time. Don't tell anybody else. Take county road three south of town, right off Main, okay? Go two miles on that, make a right at the first crossing, a left at the next. You'll see a white farmhouse about a rod beyond the left turn. It's set back about a quarter of a mile. There's a front stoop but no steps and a burnt barn out back of it. You park your heap by that barn and head north in the cornfield there. It's uphill. You go to the top. When Bo's satisfied you're alone he'll show up. You just stand there in the cornfield till he comes. Play like you're a scarecrow."

"Is Alma with him?"

"You'll find out."

"Anything happens to her, Arlo, I'll find you."

"Well, I'll worry about that a whole lot." He hung up.

Evangeline came up to the step as I charged out. I told her I was rounding up a posse and ignored her questions as I took off at a run.

I scrambled into Cody's Chevy and headed south. The sky was pale, the sun glaring, and the prairie wind swept my dust tail off across the fields as I rattled over the graveled road. The turnoff was a dirt surface and I fought the wheel to keep the wind from blowing me off it. The second turn put me on a rut road. All around me was dry corn and burned wheat fields. The road had been so rarely traveled grass and weeds brushed the front bumper and ironweed scraped on the fenders. I bounced and jounced along and finally saw the farmhouse Arlo described. It was on a low knoll and had no windbreak row of trees along the north that smart farmers choose or plant in South Dakota. It just stood there, stark naked in the wind with its empty windows, peeling paint, and bare gray wood spots. The tombstone of a dead farm.

I drove across the slope and up beside the charred remains of a small barn. It had burned long ago. Rare rain and regular sun had left little more than hints of what had been. I set the emergency brake and looked toward the hill covered with dried cornstalks which rustled in the sighing wind. I considered going through the ghost house, rejected the notion, and got out to follow Arlo's directions.

The slope was easy, the ground hard and mostly bare. I entered the corn rows and grasshoppers whirred and flew about me. The stalks were barely shoulder high. I looked over them and tried to peer through but could see nothing. Bo could be anywhere on the hill if he chose to squat. My steps were light on the earth and made little sound.

At the hill crest I paused to look around. The farmhouse was south at the edge of a shallow valley. Another farmhouse stood about a mile away to the east. It still had its barn and the traditional windbreak, which had been decimated by drought. I looked east and west across the outstretched cornfields. The country road was in view, with its telephone poles and thin, black wires swinging gently in the prairie wind. I looked back at the farmhouse.

The back door opened and a man came out. He gazed up at me, moved into the yard, and turned his head slowly, taking in the whole countryside. The wind ruffled his stiff dark hair and the collar of his denim shirt. He looked tall and rangy. Even from that distance I could see he had huge hands. In the right one he carried a hoe. He stopped for a moment, then looked at me once more. I thought he smiled.

He walked over to the Chevy and looked inside. Then he smashed the windshield with a sudden, vicious swing. The crash made a small sound in the big space around us. The wind sighed a little louder.

He started up the hill.

I moved to the nearest cornstalk and jerked it from the earth. It felt dry and hard. The leaves were stiff and rustled as I handled the stalk.

Bo moved through the corn toward me.

When he was a dozen yards away I called, "Where's Alma?"

"In the well."

"Is it dry?"

"I didn't check."

Despite the burning sun on my head and shoulders, I suddenly felt chilled, stiff, and old.

He kept coming. Once he entered the corn rows I couldn't see his hoe. He probably couldn't see my corn stalk either, but I suspected even if he'd noticed, it wouldn't have scared him any.

He wasn't in my row, so he'd have to move diagonally through half a dozen rows before we met. I ducked low and slipped through four rows, heading his way. When I straightened we were less than six feet apart. My nearness startled him. I saw his shoulders twitch as he gripped the hoe with both hands and lifted it clear of the stalks. The freshly sharpened blade gleamed silver in the sunlight. He took a short step closer. I kept my cornstalk low. He watched me with dark eyes under black brows. His tanned and leathery hide stretched tight across bony cheeks and the hard angle of his jutting jaw. There was a light in his eyes I've seen in mean kids pulling wings off of flies.

He feinted a swing, and when I only swayed, tried two more. I feinted a backward step and he lunged forward, swinging the hoe, and met the roots of the cornstalk I jabbed into his face. It caught him in the mouth, nose, and eyes, all at once. He tried to scream, the hoe went over my back, and I followed through, tumbling him backwards. I pinned him to the earth and jabbed, jabbed, jabbed. He rolled, cracking off stalks under him that popped like dead branches. My stalk broke, leaving a jagged edge which I kept driving into his head and neck. He scrambled to his knees and caught my foot in his ribs, fell to his side, and I kicked his belly and then his kidneys as he rolled again.

It took longer than I'd have believed. He finally couldn't crawl and then he couldn't twitch and then he died. I stood over him, shaking like the cornleaves in the wind and panting like a winded dog. I knelt down and felt for the pulse in his neck. My hands slipped in blood from his mouth and nose, but I made sure there was no pulse beat and then got up and ran for the well.

26

When I brought Alma back to Toqueville, Doc Leigh examined her and tried to convince me it had been fortunate there'd been no water in the well because death by a broken neck was much quicker than drowning. I couldn't quite feel grateful to Providence or God for that.

It had taken longer than growing up to get down the damned hole and bring her out. I drove back to town with the wind in my face through the shattered windshield and tried to think of anything but my passenger. I thought about Arlo and Cody and how I might manage to kill both of them. I even thought it'd be lovely to kill Bo again, but somehow the bloody thoughts didn't give me any satisfaction. Mostly, down deep, I tried to convince myself Doc Leigh could make Alma alive again.

The judge arrived while I was sitting in Annabelle's living room and said Al Jacobsen would be around soon. He asked was I sure Bo wouldn't get away?

I looked at him too long and he began to twitch.

"We don't want him to escape," he said nervously.

"He's not going anywhere," I said. I looked at him some more, wondering why Alma hadn't seemed to like him, and tried to convince myself little kids don't always get people pegged right.

"You all right?" asked the judge.

"A little tired," I said.

"Well, we'll have to go out there and get Bo where you left him. You willing to lead us?"

I was.

Al showed up a couple minutes later with his deputy in a panel truck and they followed me and the judge in Cody's car. It was a lot shorter trip than the first time even though I didn't hurry any. When we turned in at the farm the judge remarked that this was the old Grafton place, a property he'd bought a few years back. He told me a neighbor was renting the land and farming it but what with the drought he'd probably never pay.

We walked up the hill, which made the judge puff some, and when we came to Bo's body I heard the old man suck in his breath. Al said "Jesus Christ" very softly. Neither of them looked at me, but the deputy gave me a quick, horrified glance.

There was a lot of fussing about trying to drive off flies and get the big limp carcass in the stretcher the deputy'd brought. He and Al hauled it down to the panel truck and shoved it into the back.

"What in hell did you hit him with?" Al asked me.

"A cornstalk."

I saw the deputy examining the hoe Bo had brought and the judge had carried down the hill. Its sharpened edge was dusty on one side but otherwise gleamed.

Back in town Al telephoned Aquatown and caught Purvis before he'd started back. Purvis was so fired up from all they'd learned from Sarah and Tucker that it took Al several tries before he could butt in and tell him to bring the couple back, Bo was dead.

Evidently Purvis wanted to know what had happened, but all Al said was, "Don't ask."

I went back to the hotel and stretched out.

27

The story from Bo's three pals and Sarah was fairly consistent. They said Cody Jerome hired Bo to kill Ellsworth for one thousand dollars. According to Mac, who was the principal confidant, Cody wanted to marry Winnie, who he figured was a double heiress through her own parents and her in-laws. Things went sour when Cody didn't have the cash on hand for his payoff; like usual, he was betting on the come. Bo got mad, which was always his big specialty, and began a campaign of terrorizing Cody, who managed to scrape up two hundred dollars and promised faithfully to deliver the remaining eight hundred within six months. When he failed to follow through, Bo decided he'd been lying about the big money to come and resumed the harassment, which climaxed that night in Cranston when he'd made Sarah flirt with Cody, then pretended she was his girl and called Cody out. Cody'd ducked the fight, but the gang caught up with him on the highway and caused the accident that'd killed Winnie and the two Hendrickson boys.

When I commented to Mac that it'd been damned dumb to run his potential retirement fund into a clay bank where he could have died with the rest, Mac nodded and said of course, but playing smart was never Bo's long suit. He simply couldn't stand being crossed. If Cody'd died in the wreck, Bo wouldn't have given it a second thought. He sure didn't lose any sleep about the other deaths.

"How come he decided to marry Sarah?" I asked.

"Well, he heard she couldn't testify against him if she was his wife, and he never trusted a woman to keep her mouth shut. Tuck was sore about it all but he was too afraid of Bo to bitch any."

Of course Cody denied it all. He swore the only thing he'd done wrong was to talk with Bo one night in a beer parlor. He'd told him all about Ellsworth being a genius from a rich family and Bo kept asking questions and finally said it looked like the smartest thing Cody could do was see that the genius had a fatal accident. Then Cody could marry the girl and get all her money when the father-in-law croaked.

"Where I really went wrong," Cody told us confidentially, "was I told him Ellsworth was drinking himself to death anyway. Old Bo grinned and said I'd be doing the lush a favor if I killed him. I told him flat, I could never do a thing like that. He said don't worry, I'll handle it for you. Two weeks later I heard about Ellsworth being hit by the train. The next morning old Bo drove around and said I owed him. At first I thought he was kidding. But he told me all about it—how he'd hung around with Ellsworth that last night near closing time and then walked him home. He said he'd figured he'd knock him out and drive over him with his car so it'd look like an accident. Only he heard the train coming a long ways off and figured that'd be lots better, so he stalled Ellsworth till it came close. He said Ellsworth just staggered around, chuckling until there at the last moment when he realized what was happening and his mouth popped open and he tried to yell or say something but the sound of the train was too loud to hear him and then *splat!* The corner of a boxcar hit him and he just exploded. Bo said blood hit his cheek and ear, hot as fire, and splattered his shirt. He said he'd show me if I didn't believe him. But I believed him, all right. It's just the way he'd do."

Neither Al Jacobsen nor Tom Purvis believed Cody's story and he was brought to trial for murder. Brundage hired a lawyer from the Cities, a man named Samuelson. He was a tall, broad man with a wide mouth, a squashed nose, and not a lot of hair. His voice came from lower than a Texas well and it hypnotized the ladies and sort of glazed the men. He walked back and forth before the jury box, mostly with his hands behind his back, now and then waving his right hand, which held his eyeglasses that had gold rims and never got put on. His opening argument went like this:

"The prosecution'll tell you Cody Jerome was an ambitious and subtle man who hired a murderous lout to kill his mistress's husband so he could marry her and inherit a fortune. The prosecution will claim that before killing Ellsworth, who he'd called his friend, Cody had cuckolded him. Forgive me, but we must call a spade a spade since we are dealing with brutal facts. Bo Grummen's cohorts, who are not exactly model citizens by their own admission, will be paraded before you, as if they were reliable sources, telling you tales of conspiracy to commit murder.

"Now, let us get to the facts. Yes, Cody Jerome is an ambitious young man. He was born dirt-poor, his mother took in washing, and he worked and wanted from early childhood. But he has worked, remember that, and been successful in his modest way. Back when he first met the Andersons and their genius employee, those people were

as exotic to him as peacocks and champagne. He hung
about them, got himself hired to do odd jobs, one summer even worked as their lawn boy and assistant gar-
dener. Later he went on to other enterprises, but all the
while kept in touch with those people and won their trust
and friendship. And yes, he eventually did impregnate
Winnie Ellison, who had married the genius employee in
the vain hope of reforming him. But Cody planted that
child with the full knowledge and consent of Ellsworth,
who was, unfortunately, impotent. We have proof of that
and will present it to you in due time.

"Ellsworth convinced his friend Cody that the only
way Winnie could ever receive anything from her rich in-
laws was to have a baby—to present them with a
grandchild. I won't try to tell you that Cody didn't
succumb to this questionable proposition without eager-
ness. Certainly he was fascinated by the young lady from
the first time he saw her, so it is not surprising he agreed
to help defraud the elder Ellisons. And yes, he wanted to
marry her and claim his natural daughter after Ellsworth
was dead. But he did not kill Ellsworth, nor did he hire
Bo Grummen to do the deed. None of the witnesses in
this case claim they were present when the offer was
made. None saw money paid over. Bo told them all they
think they know and he lied. He was a murderous, lying
villain who slaughtered Ellsworth, Winnie, the Hendrickson brothers, and that beautiful, lovely child, Alma,
as if they were vermin. There's no record of Cody Jerome
ever committing any sort of violent crime. None. Yes,
you may find him guilty of adultery, but this trial involves
murder, which, I'm sure we all agree, is a totally
different matter."

I'm not sure the jury bought all of that but they did

agree there was no clear case made against Cody that proved he agreed to pay in advance for Ellsworth's killing, and he walked out of the court free as a jaybird.

Before all of that there was the funeral. Reverend Kronkite spent a good part of his sermon on the subject of evil and named Bo Grummen as the essence of it all. He said the slaughterer of the little Ellison family had murdered wisdom, beauty, and innocence. I tried to imagine the Lutheran minister dealing with Ellsworth's atheism, Winnie's free-sex notions, and Alma's fables. I guessed he might have managed with Alma but figured ten minutes with either of the other two would have had him ready for a straitjacket.

I'd worried some about how I could handle things when he started talking about Alma, but he lost me early on. The son of a bitch, who at most had only seen her a couple times, talked as if he'd been her mother, father, and guardian angel all the days of her short life. What he did was use her to impress the biggest crowd he'd ever had and he laid on style with a shovel. It made me sick.

I left the church in my mind and thought of ways I might corner Arlo Fisher and stomp the shit out of him. There were two things wrong with that: first, if I started I wouldn't be able to stop; and second, it didn't seem likely there'd be any satisfaction in it. Arlo was just a dumb turd and I couldn't change that by stomping his brains out. All that killing could do for me was accomplished when I did Bo in. I was glad I'd done it, and would do it again, but finishing him pretty much cleaned the spite out of me.

My last meeting with Evangeline wasn't much. I had dinner at the Leighs' and couldn't figure out from her attitude whether her sullenness came from guilt she felt about not watching Alma closer, or if she'd begun to feel embarrassed that she'd let people think she was interested in a bum like me.

Annabelle began by trying to make the supper an occasion, a farewell party even. But her cheerfulness was forced and I could see Doc Leigh getting more and more uncomfortable and glancing my way with his sad look. About halfway through the meal Annabelle suddenly got up and headed for the stairs in tears. Doc apologized, saying she was still upset about everything, and got up to follow her.

After a couple awkward moments Evangeline said, "You should have just left town."

I agreed and got up to do it. She followed me, and we walked along the dusky street for nearly a block without speaking.

"Don't gloom around," she finally said. "Think of the positive side. You came out pretty well, all things considered."

I said I didn't see it that way.

"Well, that's understandable. You didn't get me the way you planned, but you worked for the two most important men in town and you ran down and killed the bogeyman and now you're leaving town as free and unfettered as when you came."

"That bother you a lot?"

She stopped and clutched my arm. "It wasn't my fault she got killed. She'd never have died if you hadn't come to town. Someone would have got her out of the car besides you and she would've been cared for. If I'm to blame, so are you, so don't try to put it all on me."

I stared at her, seeing the tears in her eyes, and shook

my head. "I never figured you were to blame, never said anything—"

"You think it. I can see it in your eyes and know it the way you've just ignored me ever since that day. Like I was dirt or something worse. You think I'm a tease and too scatterbrained to care, but I loved her too—"

All of a sudden she was crying and she turned and started stumbling back toward the house. It was easy to keep up with her but hard to make her stop. When I managed it, she hung on to me. I wished I were the kind of guy who had a clean hanky for such an occasion but I didn't, so I wasn't much help except for support and warmth.

Pretty soon the flood let up and she found her own hanky in a pocket and mopped her cheeks and eyes and said she must look a fright and I kissed her forehead and she said I could aim better than that so I did.

We walked most of the night and talked and when the false dawn came I headed her home. I thought she might invite me up to her room and was working hard to figure how the judge would accept that, but it was no problem because we parted at the front door. She made me promise to come back and I said I would to keep her from thinking I blamed her, but I never made it.

In the morning I got my Model T out of Simpson's Garage and drove back to Corden. Somehow, just then, it seemed like the only place to go.